THE PERFECT GIFT

by

SERENITY WOODS

ISBN-13: 978-1522907978
ISBN-10: 1522907971

DEDICATION

To Tony & Chris, my Kiwi boys.

CONTENTS

Chapter One...1

Chapter Two..11

Chapter Three...19

Chapter Four..24

Chapter Five..29

Chapter Six...37

Chapter Seven...44

Chapter Eight...51

Chapter Nine..58

Chapter Ten...63

Chapter Eleven..69

Chapter Twelve..74

Chapter Thirteen..80

Chapter Fourteen..86

Chapter Fifteen...94

Chapter Sixteen..101

Chapter Seventeen..107

Chapter Eighteen...114

Chapter Nineteen...120

Chapter Twenty...127

Chapter Twenty-One...134

Chapter Twenty-Two...140

Chapter Twenty-Three...146

Chapter Twenty-Four..151

Chapter Twenty-Five..159

Chapter Twenty-Six...165

Sneak Peek at Chapter One of An Ideal Present.............171

Newsletter...179

About the Author...180

Chapter One

It was early December, supposedly the start of summer in New Zealand, but clouds had covered the sky for weeks, and spring still gripped the country with cold, gray fingers.

Brock's waterfront apartment was as dark, cool, and unwelcoming as a mortuary. He dropped his keys onto the table by the door and stood with hands on hips for a moment, hanging his head.

Two years ago, he would have been walking into his house on the outskirts of Auckland. He could still picture it—the living room glowing with Christmas lights, Fleur in the kitchen, making mince pies and singing carols, his dog curled up in his basket, soaking up the last dregs of sunlight.

Jeez, how much life could change in twenty-four months. His wife had finally succumbed to the cancer that had tortured her for years, and then—shortly afterward, as if from a broken heart—his dog had also died.

Brock was left with a depressing apartment, a cold bed, and the prospect of a microwave meal to look forward to.

Life truly sucked.

He blew out a breath and massaged the bridge of his nose. He'd fought against the despair that had threatened to overwhelm him for two years, but it continued to cling to him, like a piece of plastic wrap he couldn't shake off no matter how hard he tried.

Dispiritedly, he walked across to the large windows overlooking the City of Sails. On a Saturday night, the waterfront was always busy, and tonight so near to Christmas was no exception, the streets of Princes Wharf filled with couples and groups on their way out for the evening. Reflections of the red, gold, and blue lights from the restaurants and clubs shimmered on the water like sequins. Half of him wanted to go down and join the throng of partygoers, force himself to shake off his depression. The other half wanted never to set foot out of his apartment again.

Of all nights, he supposed, the anniversary of his wife's death would be the most likely to break through the iron barrier he'd erected around his heart and emotions. As he wasn't on call, he was going to allow himself the luxury of a fair portion of a bottle of Islay malt whisky and some melancholic playing of his guitar before he passed out on the sofa. But he wouldn't succumb to his grief completely. Fleur wouldn't have wanted him to. For that reason, if nothing else, he wouldn't give in.

So he switched on a few lamps throughout the apartment to give it a warm glow, changed out of his suit into a sweatshirt and a pair of tracksuit bottoms, put some folksy jazz on his iPod, and stared into the fridge for a whole minute as he decided what to have for dinner.

His heart told him to cook something healthy, while his tired brain demanded he stick a frozen ready meal in the microwave. He compromised by taking out of the freezer a portion of spaghetti Bolognese he'd made a few weeks ago, and reheating it. While he waited for the microwave to ping, he tipped half a bag of prepared salad onto the plate and poured a glass of red wine. After adding the pasta to the plate when it was done, he took it and the glass to his favorite chair by the window.

For a while he just ate, looking down at the lights and the people, letting his mind and body settle after his busy day. The Bolognese wasn't bad and the wine warmed him through, and he began to relax for the first time that day as the alcohol threaded through his veins.

After a while, he leaned forward and picked up his laptop from the table, balanced it on the arm of the chair, and opened it up.

As chief consultant pediatrician at Auckland Hospital, he always had a batch of emails waiting in his inbox, but as he scanned through the twenty or so messages currently sitting there unread, he decided they could all wait until the next day.

Shoveling another forkful of spaghetti into his mouth, he paused the cursor over the icon of a crown on his desktop. He debated whether to load up the forum for We Three Kings, the charity side of the business he ran with his brothers making medical equipment for children. The website had online forums and chat rooms for concerned parents to talk to each other about their sick kids. They could also ask questions of the group of doctors who volunteered spare time to help out. Barely a day went by when Brock didn't go on there, but he wasn't sure he had the energy tonight.

At that moment, a message popped up on Skype.

Yo bro. Wassup?

His lips curving, Brock clicked the call button and waited for his brother to answer. The button went green, and Charlie King's face appeared on the screen. As always, he wore an All Blacks rugby top, and his longish hair looked as if he hadn't brushed it in a week. Which, knowing Charlie, he probably hadn't.

"'Yo bro, wassup?'" Brock quoted. "You sound like a parent singing along to his son's rap music."

"I was trying to sound cool," Charlie said, taking off his glasses to clean them.

"It didn't work."

Charlie slid his glasses back on. "There's always a first time."

Brock gave a short laugh. Their upper class English mother had been determined her boys would speak "properly." As a result, although they all had a hint of a Kiwi accent, their diction was more refined than rough. Add the fact that Charlie had no interest in anything to do with popular culture and didn't even own a TV, and it made the notion of him sounding cool amusing to say the least. Luckily, Brock thought, his brother had about forty-five IQ points on most people, otherwise he would have been a hopeless case.

Charlie took a swig from the bottle of beer in his hand. "What are you up to?"

"About to down half a bottle of a forty-year-old Laphroaig."

Charlie snorted and opened his mouth to say something, but at that moment Skype pinged again showing another caller. "Hold on," Brock said, "I'll add Matt to the call."

Another window popped up with their younger brother's face. "Evening," Matt said. His hair also looked as if he'd just rolled out of bed, but Brock knew it would have taken his brother thirty minutes to achieve the same look of casual indifference that Charlie managed with no work at all.

"I'm about to convince Brock to save his forty-year-old Laphroaig until we meet up," Charlie told him. "He said he's going to down it himself tonight, but after the first two glasses he won't remember the rest and it'll be a waste."

"Damned straight," Matt said. "Stick to the ten-year-old and save the forty for Christmas Eve."

Brock grinned. "Fair enough." Their father had instilled in them all a love for a good Scotch. Brock was hosting a party on Christmas Eve in a vain attempt to encourage some Christmas spirit in himself, and he guessed it was as good a night as any to share the whisky with his brothers.

"So how's it going?" Matt settled back, sketchpad in hand, and began to doodle as they talked.

Brock shrugged. "Only just got in." He checked the clock in the corner of the screen and his eyebrows rose. Ten p.m.? He hadn't realized it was quite that late. No wonder he was hungry.

"That's late even for you," Charlie commented.

"There was a case in emergency that took a while to sort, and then I had to hand over to the night staff." Because he specialized in respiratory diseases, the emergency staff called Brock whenever children came in with breathing difficulties. Kids always seemed to get sicker in the evenings, so it wasn't unknown for him to be there until well after dark.

"What are you doing now?" Charlie asked.

"Talking to you."

Matt gave a wry smile while Charlie rolled his eyes and said, "I meant what are you going to do after you hang up?"

"I told you—down half a bottle of whisky and pass out on the sofa. I'm not on call tonight."

Charlie ran his hand through his hair, and Matt scratched his cheek with his pencil.

Brock smiled. They were concerned about him but didn't know what to say. "It's all right, guys, I'm okay. Yeah, it's a crappy day, but I'll get through it." He decided to change the subject before he started sniveling. "Hey, Charlie, what's this about Ophelia resigning?"

His brother's eyes widened. "What?"

"You didn't know?"

"No, I didn't know. Who told you?"

"One of the nurses. She gave her notice yesterday. She'll be leaving in the New Year."

Ophelia Clark was in charge of *Te Karere Hauora*, the department that connected the hospital with the local community, including the volunteers who ran the hospital radio. Brock had a sneaky feeling that Charlie had a thing for her, which was confirmed by the shocked look on Charlie's face.

"Why's she leaving?" Brock asked him.

"I've no idea."

"I thought you two talked."

"We meet at the breakfast cart in the morning. Job satisfaction doesn't tend to feature when you're discussing whether to have a blueberry muffin or a bagel."

"I thought you liked her," Matt said.

"I do."

"Have you asked her out?"

"No."

"Why not?"

"Because she's married," Charlie stated.

"Not anymore. They separated about six months ago."

Charlie's eyebrows rose so fast that Brock had to hide a smile. "What? How did I not know that?" Charlie asked.

"Everyone was talking about it," Matt said. "I assumed you knew."

"Is Summer okay?" Charlie was referring to Ophelia's daughter, who was also Brock's patient. The six-year-old girl suffered from Cystic Fibrosis and came into the hospital for intravenous antibiotics and other treatment from time to time.

"She's living with Ophelia, I think," Matt said. "I have a feeling she might have jacked the job in so she can focus more on her daughter."

They were all silent for a moment. Brock himself had given Ophelia all the platitudes after he'd diagnosed Summer—the medical world was progressing all the time, new cures were always being invented, survival rates had quadrupled over the last century… But Matt and Charlie were as aware as he was that the average life expectancy of CF sufferers was only between thirty-seven and fifty in the developed world.

He was hopeful that medical research would continue to advance that figure, though. Charlie had recently requested extra funding from

Three Wise Men for a new research project into CF, which Brock had been certain had something to do with Ophelia and her daughter.

"Ask her to the party," Brock said.

Matt snorted. "It would mean having a conversation with a woman that wasn't about muffins. Charlie doesn't do conversation about real stuff."

"Damn straight," Charlie said.

Brock rolled his eyes. "You're six-foot-four, smart, mildly amusing, and rich as Croesus. How come you're so bad with women?"

"Practice."

The other two laughed. "Ask her," Matt said with more kindness than he usually had in his voice. "What have you got to lose?"

"My dignity?"

"What dignity?"

Charlie blew out a breath. "Good point."

Brock chuckled and promised himself he'd call Charlie in the morning to talk him into it. "What about you?" He directed the question at Matt. "Are you bringing anyone?"

Matt's expression turned gloomy. "Probably not."

"Georgia still resistant to your advances?" Brock knew Matt had his eye on the girl who ran the Northland office of their business.

"I don't know about resistant—more like immune. I've tried everything."

"I didn't know there was such a thing as a woman who was impervious to your charms," Charlie said.

Matt scratched his cheek. "Neither did I." Of the three of them, Matt was the only one who could have been considered a womanizer, and his girlfriends rarely lasted longer than a few months before he got bored and broke up with them. He'd been after Georgia for ages, but Brock wasn't sure whether he was truly crazy about her, or if he only wanted her because he couldn't have her.

"Have you asked her to the party?" Brock queried.

"Yep."

"What did she say?"

"Nope."

Brock grinned. "Keep trying." He sighed. "I thought it would be reassuring to know I won't be the only sad loser this Christmas, but it makes me kinda sad."

Charlie cleared his throat. "Have you been on the forums this evening?"

"Not yet. Not sure if I have the energy."

"You should," Matt said. "Ryan's in hospital again."

Brock placed his plate on the nearby table with a clatter and sat up. "Erin's boy? Shit. What happened?"

"Another asthma attack. Don't know much more than that—she left a brief message on the asthma thread. I think she was looking for you."

"Fuck." Brock leaned back and frowned. About a year ago, he'd started talking to a young mum called Erin on one of the forums. Her son had been hospitalized after having an asthma attack, and she'd wanted to tell them that the revolutionary inhaler they'd developed had saved Ryan's life.

Through Three Wise Men, the guys developed medical equipment designed with babies and young children in mind. Charlie had invented a more effective asthma inhaler with Brock's help, and they'd decorated it with the Ward Seven characters from Matt's series of children's books. It had proved so popular that Charlie and Brock had since invented a whole range of medical equipment featuring Ward Seven toys, such as tiny animals that could be clipped onto pulse oximeters to encourage the children to sit still while they were being monitored.

Brock had talked to Erin online frequently since then. In the beginning, they'd mostly spoken about ways to manage childhood asthma, but over the months they'd taken to messaging most days. Although their chat had turned a bit more personal, it hadn't quite stepped over the line to become intimate, but she had a good sense of humor, and he rather liked her.

"Okay. I'll go on now." He pulled the computer onto his lap.

"Before you go," Charlie said, "just checking you're still on for the Ward Seven December tour tomorrow?"

Brock chuckled. Although the travelling could be tiring, he enjoyed their visits to the children's hospitals. "Yeah. Waikato for me."

"The Coromandel for me, and I think Matt's at Whangarei," Charlie replied.

"Yep." Matt nodded. "Talking of which, I've been working on a new Ward Seven character. What do you think?" He turned his sketchpad around to show his brothers. He'd drawn a possum with bulging eyes and a dopey smile. "I'm going to call him Squish," Matt said, presumably referring to the fact that possums tended to be seen only when flattened on the middle of the road.

They both laughed. "Terrific," Charlie said.

Brock agreed, then said, "Okay, I'm signing off. Speak later."

"See ya," Matt replied.

"Stay loose," Charlie said. "You know where we are if you need us."

"Yeah. Catch you online." Brock ended the call.

He double-clicked on the crown icon and loaded up the forum.

The brothers had been relatively wealthy even before they'd opened their business, but they'd been so successful that a few years ago they'd started the We Three Kings Foundation. Through the Foundation they granted wishes for children with life-threatening illnesses, as well as running a twenty-four-hour online help center for parents with sick kids.

Brock often helped out the doctors by answering questions in the online medical chat room, while Matt chatted to parents and sometimes the kids as well in the Ward Seven chat room. All three of them had worked hard to make the Foundation a success, including dressing up as Ward Seven characters and visiting children's hospitals to deliver vital medical equipment as well as more fun gifts for the patients.

The guys had started using pseudonyms on the forums in an attempt to remain anonymous, although that had flown out of the window when the New Zealand Herald had done a feature on them announcing that the creator of the famous *The Toys from Ward Seven* books was one of the three brothers behind the We Three Kings Foundation, but they'd continued to use their pseudonyms anyway.

Brock logged in as Balthasar like he always did, and pulled up the front page to see what new threads were there. His eyebrows rose as he saw one titled "Hugs for Balthasar," created by Charlie under his pseudonym, Caspar. Brock clicked on it and read the opening post.

Today is the second anniversary of the passing of Balthasar's wife. If anyone wants to send him an e-hug, feel free to do so here—I'm sure he'd appreciate it.

Charlie had finished with a smiley face.

Brock stared at the replies beneath. There were a hundred and seventy two, and it had only been up a few hours. Scrolling down, he read every one, his throat tightening the more he read. The messages were filled with thank yous from grateful parents saying how the new asthma inhaler had saved their children's lives, as well as from many explaining how the Ward Seven decorated equipment made their kids' visits to the hospital a much more pleasant experience, to the extent that sometimes the children couldn't wait to go for their checkups because they got to play with the toys. All the messages sent hugs and kisses and best wishes for him on such a difficult day.

His eyes stung, and he put the laptop to one side and rose to pour himself a whisky—following his brothers' advice and choosing the ten-year-old malt and not the forty. He took a big swallow and welcomed the burn of it down into his stomach, looking out at the lights on the harbor through blurred eyes. He thought about Fleur and how proud she'd be of him, and then he thought about his sister, Pippa, who'd died of an asthma attack when he was fourteen, and who was the main reason he'd become a doctor.

He'd been lucky enough never to have to worry about money, but money couldn't buy love, and it couldn't buy life either.

So much of his life had been about loss. Didn't he deserve some happiness? He looked down moodily at a couple standing under a street lamp, kissing. What he wouldn't give to have a woman's arms around him tonight.

Then he blinked and caught his breath at the thought, guilt flooding him. What a thing to think on the anniversary of Fleur's death. He'd promised himself he'd never look at another woman again, let alone date or fall in love. For two years he'd been celibate and had barely given women a second thought. He'd loved Fleur with all his heart, and when she'd died, his heart had not only broken but had shattered into so many pieces he'd thought he'd never be able to fit them all back together again.

But for the first time, Brock acknowledged to himself that he was lonely.

You left me, he thought, looking up at the star-studded sky. *You left me alone, and I miss you, and I've tried to go on by myself, but I'm only human.*

Six months after Fleur had died, friends had started inviting him out on dates, but he'd refused every suggestion of meeting someone. He'd grieved for two years. Was it disloyal to feel he was finally ready to move on?

He ached to feel a warm body against him, and to feel the shared bliss of sexual release, but equally it wasn't just about that. He missed talking to Fleur, telling her his hopes and fears, and just knowing someone was there for him. That kind of love came around only once in a lifetime, but if someone else existed who could provide even a fraction of the joy he'd felt with his first wife, he knew he would be a lucky man.

Glancing at the laptop still resting on the arm of the chair, he thought about Erin. He had no idea what she looked like, where she lived, or much about her private life, apart from that she was a single parent and had a young son. But he liked her, and she made him laugh. Was that so terrible?

He shouldn't talk to her. Maybe another night he could have a chat, but tonight wouldn't be right. Would it?

What would Fleur say? He could almost hear her voice, a little impatient, slightly amused. *Her boy's in hospital, Brock. For God's sake, just talk to the woman.*

His lips curved up, and he went back to the chair and pulled the laptop toward him.

Chapter Two

Erin shifted onto her back on the tiltaway bed and looked up at the ceiling. The Christmas fairy lights strung around the hospital ward glowed in the semi-darkness, the tinsel glittering where it caught the light.

It was only ten o'clock, but she hadn't slept at all the previous night, and her eyes were scratchy with tiredness. For some reason, though, they refused to shut, and images continued to flitter through her overactive brain.

Actually, now she came to think about it, she felt as if she hadn't had more than a few hours' sleep a night since Ryan was born. Until he was eighteen months, he'd kept her awake half the night with his constant coughing, but repeated trips to the doctor had resulted in antibiotics at the best, or being told it was a virus and there was nothing they could do at the worst. One doctor had offered a half-hearted diagnosis of possible asthma and had given her an inhaler with a children's breathing mask, but he'd not shown her how to use it, and Ryan had made such a fuss when she tried that in the end she'd given up.

It had taken a full blown asthma attack and hospitalization for her to come to terms with the fact that he truly had asthma, and to learn how to treat it in a way that was safe and stress-free for both her and Ryan. He hated the nebulizer, but the doctor at Three Wise Men has reassured her that using an inhaler with a spacer was just as effective when used regularly, and Ryan didn't mind using that because he could play with the Dixon the Dog toy that clipped on the side. But she hadn't slept soundly since, terrified she'd wake up to find he'd had an asthma attack in the night and she hadn't heard him. As it happened, his most recent attack had started mid-morning after a few days of developing a respiratory infection, but she doubted she'd sleep any easier because of it.

Here in the hospital, she knew she shouldn't be worrying because the nurses were monitoring him, but even so, it was difficult to stop a habit when it involved whether your child lived or died.

She pushed herself up to a sitting position and peered over the adjacent bed. Ryan slept on his side facing her, his lashes dark against his pale cheek. He had an IV in his hand administering hydrocortisone. His other chubby little hand clutched the paw of the Dixon the Dog toy clipped to the tube beneath the mask over his face. The Ward Seven toys played a huge part in comforting Ryan when he had to take his medication.

Swallowing hard, she lay back and stared up at the ceiling again. She wasn't going to cry.

Gritting her teeth, she picked up her phone and brought up the We Three Kings forums. It had grown to mean much more to her than a place to get medical advice. She'd made many friends on the forums and chat rooms who were in a similar position to herself with sick children, and they all provided support and comfort for each other when things got tough.

She'd seen the message from Caspar earlier. It was the first time she'd realized that Balthasar—the doctor she'd conversed with in the past—had lost his wife two years ago. She'd joined in with everyone else in sending her thoughts and wishes, but he hadn't appeared, and she knew he would probably have other things on his mind tonight.

To her surprise, though, he'd recently been on and replied to the messages on the forum.

Hi everyone, he'd written. *Thank you so much for all your kind wishes. I appreciate every one of you for taking the time to write. Fleur died two years ago after a long battle with breast cancer. I miss her every day, and of course anniversaries are always difficult, so it's lovely to read all your messages. The Foundation was her idea, and she understood that communication and support are key in dealing with sickness. She would be thrilled to know how much these forums have grown. I'm glad that I, Caspar, and Melchior have been able to help people in even a little way.*

His words had already been followed by a dozen messages from people reiterating their best wishes and saying how We Three Kings was the only thing that had gotten them through a difficult time.

She was just about to add another comment when a direct message box popped up.

Evening, Erin. I understand that Ryan is back in hospital—so sorry to hear that. I'm sure you're busy, but if you want to talk, I'm here.

Her eyes widened as she saw it was from Balthasar.

She'd talked a lot with him the first time Ryan had been hospitalized. She'd been terrified and, as she didn't have asthma herself, she hadn't really understood the ins and outs of the disease. Although the hospital staff had been patient and kind, Balthasar had answered every tiny question she'd had, suggesting many medical and alternative therapies for dealing with asthma, as well as reassuring her that, providing it was well-managed, it didn't have to be debilitating for the child.

Their relationship—if you could call it that—went deeper than medical help, though. There was no way she could be sure, but she suspected he didn't have the time to talk to every person on the forums for as long as he talked to her.

Smiling, conscious of her heart picking up its pace a little, she tapped the reply box.

Good evening Balthasar, she typed. *Lovely to hear from you.*

It was only seconds before another message popped up. *Hey, Erin. How are you and Ryan doing?*

He's okay, a little better. They've got him on a hydrocortisone drip and the nebulizer, and his breathing's stabilized.

Is he all right using the neb?

He didn't want to, but he got better when they clipped Dixon to it :-) Erin sighed. She'd said thank you to him so many times that she was sure he was tired of her repeating herself, but it had to be said. *Please thank Melchior and Caspar again for me if you see them. I can't explain how much difference it makes to Ryan having the Ward Seven toys with him in hospital.*

I will. I've just been speaking to them. You can tell Ryan there will be a new toy joining Ward Seven soon—a possum apparently called Squish.

Erin covered her mouth with a hand to stop herself laughing out loud. *I love it, that's wonderful.*

She paused with her finger over the keypad. Although they'd talked a lot about a variety of things, they'd rarely overstepped the boundary to deeply personal issues. Should she say something about Caspar's post?

Up on the bed, Ryan coughed, and she sat up to see whether he'd woken up, but his eyes were still closed. She bit her lip, then lay down again. Screw this, she thought. Life was too short not to take chances.

I'm sorry to hear about your wife, she typed. *That's very sad.*

For a long time, maybe around two minutes, he didn't reply. He was probably busy, she thought. Just because his wife had died didn't mean he was alone, or perhaps he'd put his computer down and wandered off.

She was just about to lay her phone to one side and try to sleep again when a message came back.

I know this is a bit unusual, and of course please say no if you feel uncomfortable, but I wondered whether you'd like to talk properly for once? I'd be happy to call you if you send me your number. But I understand if you'd rather not, and we can carry on talking like this if you wish. Or not. Whatever. I'll shut up now. An embarrassed emoticon followed.

She caught her breath, her cheeks warming. He wanted to talk to her? Her mind spun, but she scolded it for leaping to conclusions. He only wanted to make sure Ryan was okay—he'd probably talk medical matters and that would be it.

So why was she blushing?

Heart racing, she tapped reply. *I'd love to talk to you, if you're not too busy.* She finished with her mobile number, pressed send, then waited, biting her nail. The phone was already on vibrate so she didn't have to worry about waking Ryan, who could usually sleep through an earthquake anyway.

Her mouth had gone dry, and she sat up and turned around on the tiny bed so her back was against the wall. Ryan and the other boy in the ward were asleep, so she'd have to keep her voice down.

The phone vibrated in her hand, and she tapped the answer button and held it to her ear. "Hello?"

"Hi, is that Erin?" The man's voice was deep and husky, and it sent a shiver all the way down her spine.

"Yes, hello Balthasar." She felt all flustered. "It's lovely to speak to you at last."

He chuckled. "Please, call me Brock. That's my real name. The three of us use pseudonyms on the net, even though I'm sure everyone read that article in the Herald."

"What article?"

"You didn't read it? Wow, you must be the one person in the whole country. They did a feature on us—my two brothers and I. Our surname is King."

"Ah, hence the names for your company?"

"That's right. Charlie—he's Caspar on the website—suggested Three Wise Men for the name of our medical business. Matt and I weren't so sure. We thought it was just begging the press to point out all the stupid things we've done over the last few years."

Erin laughed. "I'm sure there haven't been that many."

"You'd be surprised." His voice was wry. "Hey, it's nice to talk to you at last. We should have done this much sooner."

Her face glowed again. "I know. We must have been talking online for nearly a year now."

"Yeah it was about this time last year that Ryan was first in hospital, wasn't it?"

"That's right."

"He's obviously susceptible to summer colds. I'm guessing your doctors there have suggested he has a flu shot from now on?"

"Actually, no." She hadn't thought about it either. Now he'd mentioned it, it made perfect sense. "I think they've been concentrating more on getting him better right now than on the big picture stuff."

"Fair enough, but he should have one as soon as he's better, and then every year from now on. I was thinking it's possible that his asthma might be irritated by pollen. Was there a thunderstorm where you are before his attack?"

Erin's jaw dropped. "Yes. How did you know?"

"Just a guess. Changes in air pressure can lead to the bursting of pollen grains, creating smaller particles. These carry the allergens which can be inhaled deep into the lungs. It would make sense to step up his Flixotide inhaler from August maybe to February or March. We really need to work on preventing these attacks from happening rather than curing them when they do."

"Okay, Brock, I'll think about that, thank you." She spoke rather shyly, touched he genuinely seemed to care.

He didn't reply, and she hesitated, waiting for him to say goodbye now he'd done his doctoral duty.

Instead, though, he said, "And how are you?"

She rubbed her nose. "I'm okay."

"Having a child in hospital can be incredibly stressful, I know. Have you eaten today?"

"Yes, Dad."

He laughed. "Just checking."

"My parents sat with Ryan for a while and I went down to the cafe. I wasn't hungry but I made myself eat a steak and cheese pie."

"Was it nice?"

"Not bad actually. I can't cook to save my life so anything's better than microwave meals."

He laughed again, and Erin smiled, glad she'd cheered him up. Should she broach the subject of his late wife? It seemed rude not to.

"Hey, I'm very sorry to hear you lost your wife a few years ago. That's very sad."

"Thanks." He spoke softly. "Yeah, it was tough. She'd been ill a long time."

"How are you doing? Have you eaten?"

"Yes, Mum." She could hear the smile in his voice. "Compared to some other people, I can actually cook a decent meal. I'd frozen some Bolognese that I'd cooked a few weeks ago. It wasn't bad, even reheated."

It didn't sound as if he was living with anyone. She scratched at a mark on her jeans. Why did it matter? It wasn't as if she was interested in him.

She touched the back of her fingers to her warm cheeks. *Yeah, right.*

He cleared his throat. "I hope you don't mind me asking, but I know so little about you. Is Ryan's father there with you?"

She scratched again at the mark on her jeans. "No. Jack left while I was pregnant. He wasn't interested in being a dad."

"Huh." Brock sounded distinctly unimpressed.

"Yeah. He lives in Australia somewhere—I don't know where. He doesn't want to know Ryan. He won't even pay child support." Erin swallowed. It still hurt to say the words. The authorities had tried to force him to pay, but he moved often and they had trouble keeping tabs on him. She'd long ago stopped expecting miracles.

"Christ. That's harsh." Brock's voice was sharp.

Erin blew out a breath and rested her head back on the wall. "It's more complicated than it sounds. He told me when I met him that he didn't want kids. I didn't think much about it—I just thought it was something young guys say, you know? We'd only been dating six months when I fell pregnant. He still thinks I did it on purpose, out of spite I guess. I didn't, but that doesn't matter if he doesn't believe it." Hell, why was she blurting all this out? Surely Brock wasn't interested in her life history?

But she heard the glug of liquid being poured into a glass, and then an exhalation, as if he'd returned to his chair and stretched out to relax. "There are always two sides to every story. I wouldn't presume to make judgements about your... husband?"

"We never married."

"Partner, then. But after saying that, I don't think it says much about him that he'd turn his back on his son, whatever the circumstances—or perceived circumstances—of his conception."

"Thank you." His comments warmed her from the inside out. "It's easy to think it's my fault that Ryan doesn't have a visible daddy. It's nice to hear someone say otherwise."

"Your ex doesn't see him at all?"

"Nope. It's Ryan's birthday tomorrow—nice to spend it in hospital, eh?—but Jack hasn't even sent him a present." She sighed.

Brock fell silent for a moment. Then he said, "What hospital are you in?"

"Whangarei. Why?"

"Just wondered." He didn't elaborate, and she heard the clink of ice cubes being swirled in a glass.

"What are you drinking?" she asked.

"A very nice ten-year-old Islay malt."

"Ooh. Bowmore? Ardbeg?"

"Laphroaig actually. I'm impressed. You like whisky?"

"I do. I haven't had a glass since Ryan was born, though. He doesn't sleep well and I get up several times a night. I worry that I won't hear him if I've had a drink, especially since he started having asthma attacks." She gave a long sigh. "I'd kill for a drink now though. Maybe I'll treat myself to one next weekend."

"Why, what's happening then?"

"It's my birthday."

"Oh?"

"Yes. The ripe old age of twenty-seven! Obviously it depends whether Ryan's out of hospital, but I think he'll probably be discharged tomorrow as he's doing so well. Mum wants to give me a break and said she'd stay with him once he's asleep so I can have the night off. She wants me to go away somewhere."

"Sounds like a great idea."

"Yeah, although I probably won't go. You know what it's like. The guilt weighs too heavily."

"You have to look after yourself too, Erin."

She loved the way he said her name. "I suppose."

"I mean it. We're no good to our children if we're exhausted. We all need time off to regenerate. You should take your mum up on it if she's generous enough to offer to help."

"I'll think about it." She knew she'd probably say no, though. As appealing as a night on her own in a hotel sounded, she'd only end up lying awake worrying about Ryan, and drinking on her own was rarely fun.

She yawned, and Brock laughed. "I'd better let you go to sleep. I'm sure you're shattered."

A surge of disappointment nearly made her complain like a toddler having to leave a party, but she bit her lip and just said, "Well, it was lovely to talk to you."

"Likewise. I'm glad Ryan's on the mend."

"I'm sorry about your wife, Brock."

"Thanks."

"Don't drink too much, eh?"

He chuckled. "Nah, I won't. I was planning to sit up and play some moody guitar, but you've lifted some of my melancholy. I think I'll go to bed soon, too."

"I'm glad I could help," she said sincerely. "It's the least I could do after all the times you've helped me."

"That's what I'm here for." His voice was filled with smiles. "Sleep well."

"You too."

"Night." He ended the call.

Erin slipped the phone back into the pocket of her jeans. She stood and leaned over Ryan, bent and kissed him on the cheek, then climbed back onto her bed.

Her eyelids drooped, and she turned onto her side, studying the Christmas lights through her lashes.

A smile remained on her lips until she'd drifted off to sleep.

Chapter Three

Brock had forgotten how hot the dog suit was.

That morning, the clouds that had covered the country for weeks had finally cleared, and summer had hit New Zealand with a vengeance. The children's ward of Whangarei hospital had air conditioning, but the late afternoon sun streaming through the windows felt like a blowtorch on the fur that covered him from head to toe.

Luckily, he'd been sensible enough to wear shorts but, beneath the suit, sweat ran down his back and his T-shirt stuck to his skin. Christ knew what his hair would look like when he eventually removed Dixon's head.

"Stop moaning," said the woman standing by his side. Georgia ran the Far North branch of We Three Kings, coordinating fundraising opportunities and the wishes for sick kids, and organizing the guys' visits to the hospitals. "Matt never moans like this."

"Matt absolutely moans as much as me," Brock grumbled. "It's a family trait. All the King males are renowned for it. You only think he doesn't because you're soft on him."

Even through the tiny eyeholes of the suit, he saw the way Georgia's cheeks reddened. He was right—she was soft on his brother.

But she just said, "Rubbish," turned on her heel, and walked off to the next ward.

Chuckling, Brock picked up the large sack of presents and followed her. He and Georgia had already delivered some free medical equipment to the hospital, and now it was time to help the kids. Compared to the families in the hospital, his troubles were inconsequential, and he pushed his discomfort away, ready to concentrate on the two children in the room who were sitting up in their beds, eyes wide at the sight of the real Dixon the Dog coming to visit them.

When his gaze fell on the woman standing at the side of the bed on his right, Brock stopped in his tracks. It was Erin—he knew it instinctively. How he knew, he wouldn't have been able to say. He'd had no idea what she looked like. She could have been four feet tall, weighed two hundred pounds, and had hair like a scarecrow for all he knew. Not that it would have made any difference if she had, he reminded himself. This wasn't a romantic visit—he was here because it was Ryan's birthday and he felt sorry for the boy.

Even as he thought the words, he knew he was fooling himself. He couldn't deny he was here for Erin too.

The woman whose jaw had dropped when he'd entered the room walked around the bed and stopped, staring at him with wide eyes. It had to be Erin. She looked exactly the way he'd pictured her when he'd talked to her the previous night: tall, curvy, and with blonde hair in a simple braid that hung over one shoulder. She also had a pretty face and a beautiful smile that shone as bright as the summer sun.

Wow.

Georgia looked over her shoulder and beckoned to him with a frown. He wrenched his gaze away from the woman and walked into the room.

"Hello boys," Georgia said. "Santa heard that you have both been unwell, and he's sent someone special to see you. Do you know who this is?"

"It's Dixon!" Both boys screamed in delight.

The adults in the room laughed, and Georgia grinned at Brock. "That's right," she said. Turning to look at the boy on the left, she asked, "What's your name?"

"Tom," the lad said, eyes open so wide Brock worried they might pop out and roll across the floor.

"Well, Tom, Dixon has a special present for you," Georgia said. "Would you like to see it?"

Tom bounced on the bed, clearly thrilled to meet the dog from the Ward Seven gang. Brock's throat tightened. Tom had a Carmel the Cat bracelet holding the tube going into his hand and a Koru the Kiwi attached to his pulse oximeter, while the boy opposite him— who must be Ryan—had a Dixon spacer lying on his bed and a Pepper the Pukeko hanging from his drip. He made a mental note to tell Matt, who would be thrilled to know his characters were helping kids right across the country.

Lowering the sack on his back, he reached in, pulled out one of the boxes, and took it over to Tom. The boy accepted it with an open mouth.

"Say thank you, sweetie," his mother prompted.

"Thank you," the boy mumbled, holding the box as if it were a priceless artefact.

Brock patted the boy on the head with his big paw. The box only contained a large plush Dixon, but he had no doubt that to Tom it would be more precious than gold.

Georgia moved forward, holding up her phone. "Would you like a photo taken with Dixon?" she asked Tom. "Then you can show your friends that you met him."

The boy nodded, and Brock leaned down and put his arm around him. Tom beamed, and Georgia took the shot as the adults around them laughed. "I'll get it printed and put into a nice frame, and I'll send it on to you," Georgia told Tom's mother.

Brock waved goodbye, and then it was time to move to the next patient. He walked across the floor, suddenly conscious of the huge feet he wore and hoping he didn't trip up as the young woman standing patiently beside the bed watched him approach.

"And what's your name?" Georgia asked the boy.

"Ryan," he said shyly, lifting his spacer so he could suck on the paw of the miniature Dixon.

It was Erin with him—Brock had been right. He couldn't take his eyes off her. He was only a foot away from her now, and up close she was even more beautiful than she had been from across the room. She wore faded jeans and a T-shirt that had been tie-dyed with an orange sunburst pattern, but it still didn't outshine her dazzling smile. *I should have brought sunglasses*, he thought. He wouldn't see properly again for hours.

Georgia's mouth formed an O of fake surprise. "Oh, Ryan, a little bird told me it's a very special day for you."

Ryan rose up onto his knees. He was a cute lad with dark curls, a button nose, and innocent *It wasn't me, it was like that when I got here* eyes.

"Was it Pepper?" Ryan asked.

Erin tipped her head at him. "Was what Pepper, sweetie?"

"The little bird who said it was my birthday." He pointed up at the toy clipped to his drip. "Was it Pepper the Pukeko?"

"Aw." Erin gave the sexy laugh that Brock had heard on the phone, and he was lost. For the first time in two years, he thought maybe his heart wasn't as frozen solid as he'd feared.

Georgia chuckled at Ryan's comment. "That's right, honey. Pepper told me it was your birthday today. How old are you?"

"I'm two," Ryan announced proudly.

"No sweetie, you're three now," Erin reminded him.

"Oh." Ryan looked confused. "I forgot."

"Because it's your birthday," Georgia reminded him. "You're a whole year older. And Dixon has a special something for you."

Brock held up Dixon's big paw and curled his thumb and little finger so they touched, leaving the rest of the dog's big fingers pointing up.

"Three special somethings," Georgia corrected. "What do you have in the sack, Dixon?"

He pulled out the same sized parcel he'd given to the rest of the kids in the hospital—a large, plush Dixon in a box, neatly wrapped by Georgia herself. Ryan squealed and took the box with a big "Thank you!"

Next, Brock took out a flat parcel, which was a DVD of the newest series of the cartoon TV show of Ward Seven. Ryan took the present with an open mouth.

Brock held out his hand, palm uppermost.

"How many presents do you have, Ryan?" Georgia bent and asked him.

"Two," Ryan counted, holding them up.

"And how old are you?"

He grinned—his mother's smile, bright and beaming. "Three!"

"One more present please, Dixon!" Georgia declared.

Brock pulled out the last, special parcel and gave it to Ryan. It was a large, flat box.

"Can I open it, Mummy?" the boy asked, eyes wide. Erin glanced at Brock as if asking permission.

Putting his arm around the boy, Brock tugged a little at the wrapping paper, and Ryan tore it off. He squealed at the sight of the box of Lego dinosaurs, then turned and threw his arms around Dixon.

Brock hugged him back, touched by the boy's affection, and glanced up at Erin. She was staring at them, clearly baffled as to how he knew that was what her son had been asking for. Next to her, the older woman who was presumably her mother smiled.

Ryan had his photo taken with Dixon too, and then it was time to move on to the next wards, as Georgia wanted to finish giving the children presents before their tea was served.

Brock waved goodbye to everyone and walked to the door, then stopped when he felt a hand on his arm.

"Wait." It was Erin. He turned and looked down into her bright eyes. "Um... I just wanted to say thanks," she said. She bit her lip, and he could see she was dying to ask how he knew about the Lego set.

Georgia—who was in on the whole thing—grinned at them. "Aw, does mummy want a hug from Dixon too?"

Brock chuckled and put his arms around Erin, and she laughed and hugged him as the children cheered. As a rule, he didn't speak in the Dixon costume, but he put his mouth close to her ear and murmured, "I'll be back when I've finished. Need to talk to you."

He moved away. Her eyes had widened, but he didn't wait for her to say anything, just smiled inside the suit and followed Georgia out of the room.

Chapter Four

Erin watched Dixon the Dog walk off to the next ward. Her heart hammered and the surprise had made her breathless. When he'd said those words, she'd been certain it sounded like the man she'd spoken to the night before.

Brock was here? Had he been coming all along or had he organized the event just for her?

A nurse stopped next to her and smiled at the squeals that echoed from the next ward. "That's cheered them all up," she said.

Erin cleared her throat. "Has the visit been organized for a while or was it arranged today?"

"Oh we booked it months ago," the nurse advised. "Dixon comes here every few months to give gifts to the kids."

Erin nodded, annoyed at her own disappointment. Of course he hadn't arranged it all for her. It had just been a coincidence that Ryan had been admitted the day before Brock was due to visit.

And yet how had he known about the Lego dinosaur box that Ryan had seen before he went into hospital? Erin had already bought him a box of Lego for his birthday, and he'd been delighted with it, but she'd made a mental note to get the new dinosaur box for him for Christmas. How had Brock known that, or again, was it just another coincidence?

Her mind whirling, she went back to Ryan's bed. He'd already opened the box of Lego, and her mother was helping him sort out the pieces.

"Well that was weird," Erin said. "Totally didn't expect that."

Karen Bloom looked up and winked at her daughter. "The universe has a strange way of working things out."

Erin narrowed her eyes. Her mother had a mischievous look about her that suggested she knew more about Brock's visit than she was letting on. Erin opened her mouth to ask another question, but a nurse appeared to do a series of checks and then it was teatime, so she pushed everything to the back of her mind and concentrated on her son.

She'd bought him a cake, and Karen nipped out to light the candles then brought it in while some of the nurses and the adults in the room sung him happy birthday. Erin's throat tightened as Ryan's eyes glowed and he rose to blow out the candles.

For a panicky hour the day before, his breathing had gotten so bad she'd worried he wouldn't see his birthday. Closing her eyes, she said a quick thank you prayer to the hospital, the nurses, Three Wise Men, and anyone else who might be listening for their help in saving his life.

"Ms. Bloom?"

Erin opened her eyes as she felt a hand on her arm and turned to see the pretty young woman who'd come into the ward previously with Dixon.

"Hi," the woman said. "Do you have a moment?"

Glancing at Ryan, Erin saw him busy sorting out his Lego again. Her mother flicked her fingers at her, shooing her away.

"Sure," Erin replied.

"I'm Georgia," the woman said, leading the way out of the ward and down the corridor. "Dixon wondered whether you had a minute for a quick chat."

"Oh, yes of course."

"He's in here." Georgia stopped outside a closed door. Glancing around to make sure there were no children watching, she opened the door, waited for Erin to enter, then closed it behind her.

It was a tiny office, the table at the far end stacked with papers and folders, the window above it casting late afternoon sunlight across the man in the process of removing the Dixon the Dog head of his costume. He'd already taken off the large fur paws and, as she watched, he lifted the head and tucked it under his arm.

Jaw dropping, Erin stared at him.

After he'd mentioned the Herald article on the Three Wise Men, she'd made a mental note to check him out on the internet, but when they'd finished their phone call she'd gone straight to sleep, and today she'd been so busy she hadn't had time to look him up.

She'd had no idea what he looked like. All she'd known was that she liked the sound of his voice. She would never have expected him to look so... well... gorgeous.

True, all she could see was his head, but he had short dark hair threaded with gray at the temples, warm brown eyes, and a face she could have stared at for hours without getting bored.

"We meet at last," he said, and grinned, his eyes creasing at the edges.

"Brock." She couldn't have fought the smile that spread across her face even if she'd wanted to. "How lovely to finally meet you."

He put Dixon's head into a large black bag and gestured at the rest of the costume. "I'm so hot in this outfit. You could cook muffins in it. You don't mind if I strip off, do you?"

Is the Pope Catholic? Erin shook her head. "No, of course not. Go ahead. Do you… ah… want me to turn around?" *Please, please, don't say yes.*

An impish smile curved his lips. "It's okay, I am wearing shorts." He opened a Velcro flap at the front and undid the zip. "Do you think Ryan enjoyed his surprise?"

"I know he did. He'll talk about nothing else for weeks." She tried not to stare as Brock eased the suit off his shoulders, let it drop, and stepped out of it. He hadn't lied—he wore a T-shirt and shorts underneath, but he was obviously hot because the T-shirt was soaked through and sticking to his muscular body.

Ooh.

"Yuck," he said and pulled a face. "I'm so sorry, I didn't think this through. It's not the best way to meet a lady for the first time." Grabbing the wet T-shirt at the back of his neck, he tugged it off, then gestured to a clean one hanging over the nearby chair. "Pass me that, will you? Sorry."

Wordlessly, she handed him the clean tee, trying to resist the urge to fan herself at the sight of his naked torso. Jeez, the guy had a body that made her mouth water. He wasn't ripped, exactly, but his muscles were tight and toned enough to tell her he took care of himself without standing in front of the mirror with weights every day preening.

She cleared her throat. "I'm so glad you happened to be visiting today. What a great coincidence."

Tugging on the T-shirt, he appeared oblivious to the drool she was sure must be coating her chin. He ran a hand through his hair before meeting her gaze. His lips curved up again and an embarrassed look crossed his face. "Well, ah, it wasn't that much of a coincidence.

My brother, Matt, was supposed to visit Whangarei and I was off to Waikato, but I asked him if we could swap at the last minute."

He tossed the top he'd removed into a sports bag and the rest of the costume into the black bag, then faced her, sliding his hands into the pockets of his shorts. "I hope you don't mind. I wanted to give Ryan something to cheer him up."

Warmth had flooded her cheeks so she knew she must be blushing, but she didn't look away, needing to understand how much of this was coincidence and how much he'd engineered. "How did you know he wanted that Lego?" she asked curiously.

The sheepish look returned. "I rang your mother." His brows drew together. "Actually, now I say it out loud it sounds a bit creepy. Does it help if I say I asked Georgia to track your mum down?"

"Um…" Erin didn't know what to think. He'd actually spoken to her mother? She was going to kill her for keeping that to herself. "Not really."

They studied each other for a moment. Erin was too startled to think straight. Brock looked wary, as if concerned she might accuse him of stalking her.

He glanced away for a moment, out of the window at the deep blue sky, giving Erin the opportunity to study his profile. Straight nose, sculpted lips, a touch of bristle on his cheeks. Had he really gone to all that trouble to find out who her mother was so he could buy Ryan a present? She didn't know whether to feel alarmed or incredibly touched.

Brock blew out a long breath, still looking out of the window. "The thing is, I felt sorry for Ryan being here on his birthday, and I wanted to cheer him up. That's what We Three Kings is for, making kids feel better. But that wasn't the only reason I came."

He looked back at Erin. His eyes held a warmth that heated her from the inside out. "We've talked online for a long time," he said, "and… well, I like you. I wanted to meet you. To see if you looked as gorgeous as you sounded." He smiled.

"Oh." She tried to catch her breath and failed. "Goodness." She tried to act casual, as if gorgeous rich men threw compliments at her all the time, and failed, a smile curving her lips.

"You do, by the way," he clarified. "Just so you know."

She held his gaze as long as she could, then stared at her shoes for a moment, her cheeks burning. Jeez, she was acting like she was fifteen again, but she couldn't help it. No man had talked to her like this in an ice age, if ever.

Brock chuckled. "I'm embarrassing you, I'm sorry."

"It's okay, it's nice. I'm just not used to compliments."

"I sincerely doubt that, but if it is the truth, all it tells me is that the male population of the Northland must be blind."

"Brock, stop." She covered her cheeks with her hands. "You're making me blush."

He laughed and looked at his watch. "Look, the kids are having their tea at the moment. I wondered whether you'd like to take a break and join me for a coffee in the restaurant?"

"Oh. Um…" Her mind whirled. Her mother would be happy to stay with Ryan for half an hour and he wouldn't even notice she was gone while he had his new box of Lego. "Okay, that would be nice. Thank you."

"Come on then." He gestured to the door with his head. "Georgia tells me they make a great mince pie here, and I'm starving."

Chapter Five

"So come on then." Brock sipped his piping hot coffee, trying not to burn his lip. "Tell me about yourself." He smiled at the woman sitting opposite him, who looked as if she was also trying not to burn her lip, both of them as self-conscious as if they were on a date. Which they sort of were, he supposed, even if it wasn't a very romantic one.

Erin gave a sexy shrug of her shoulders. "I think you already know everything about me."

"Aw, come on. I know all about Ryan and how you've looked after him. I don't know anything about *you*." It was true—they'd talked often about the difficulties of looking after a sick kid, but they'd never made the step across that unspoken boundary into personal details until now.

"What would you like to know?" she asked, looking genuinely puzzled.

He leaned forward on the table, wanting to know more about this mysterious woman who pressed all his buttons, though he had no idea why. "Tell me about yourself, Erin. Do you work? What music do you like? What books do you read? I want to discover the woman behind the mother."

Her smile faded, and she poked at the cream-covered mince pie on her plate with a fork. "I'm not sure there is one anymore." Her tone was wry, but he sensed a touch of despair behind it. "I've been a mum for so long I've forgotten what it's like to be me."

He nodded, took a bite of his mince pie, and ate it with enthusiasm. Georgia was right—it was terrific. "Yeah, that happens with both parenthood and demanding careers. I know sometimes I'm not home until ten, and I walk into my apartment and think right, time to myself, and I'm, like, okay… What do I do now?"

Erin laughed, her face lighting up, and Brock melted inside. He wanted to make her laugh like that all the time.

"That happens to me too," she said. "I finally persuade Ryan to have a nap or get him to bed at night, and I think great, me time, and sometimes it's all I can do to sit and watch the TV."

"That's natural," he said. "Parenting is incredibly hard. Nowadays we're all told we're supposed to be super-parents, holding down a demanding career while being a terrific mother or father and partner, and it's not that easy."

"Well I don't have a partner, I only work part-time at the local bookshop, and I'm a terrible mother, so I'm not sure what that says about me." She laughed before eating her mince pie.

"You're hardly a terrible mother, Erin. Look at all the research you've done into how to cope with an asthmatic child—not every mother can say the same. You'd be surprised."

Her eyebrows rose. "I suppose." Then an impish smile crossed her face. "But I can't cook. I mean it—somehow even when I follow a recipe it always goes wrong, probably because I'm impatient and can't be bothered to measure anything." She gave a girlish giggle that made him grin. "I can't sew," she continued, "or knit. Too impatient to learn."

"I'm sensing a theme here," he said. "Patience not your strong point?"

"Um, no. Not really. Life's too short to stuff a mushroom, you know?"

"Yeah." He smiled. "So you work in a bookshop?"

"Three mornings a week while Ryan's at playgroup. Keeps me sane. Kind of." She rolled her eyes. "I like yoga. I paint a bit, not well, terribly messy abstract stuff that doesn't mean anything to anyone but me, but I like doing it. I listen to funky rhythm and blues and jazz, and I can sing a bit. I like watching comedies that make me laugh and emotional dramas that make me cry. I love chocolate and I hate ginger. How's that?"

Brock studied her face, watching how it lit up as she talked about the things she enjoyed doing. She'd look a million dollars in a designer dress with her hair done, makeup applied, and expensive jewelry glittering at her ears and on her fingers, but equally he loved her fresh-faced look, her sheer joie-de-vivre. She obviously thought she'd lost it since becoming a mother, but it was still there, like the Christmas baubles hanging by the counter that glittered when they caught the light.

"So," she said, a light pink touching her cheekbones as he continued to watch her. "You're a consultant pediatrician at Auckland Hospital?"

"Yes. My brother Charlie works there too—he develops medical equipment. My other brother you know as Matt King—he of Ward Seven fame." He waited for her to quiz him about Matt the way most women did, captivated by the guy who was famous nationwide for his Kiwi cartoon characters.

"So what made you want to be a doctor?" she asked instead. "And a pediatrician at that?"

Warmed by her interest, he finished off his cake, pushed away the plate, and sat back in his chair. "My sister, Pippa, died when I was fourteen. She had an asthma attack. She was only eight. I was looking after her while my parents took Matt and Charlie to a school football competition. It was the middle of winter, freezing cold, but Pippa was bored and annoyed that the guys had gone to play football without her, so I took her into the garden for a kick around."

It was still surprisingly difficult to talk about it, even after all these years. Brock concentrated on the table, picking at a black mark on the plastic with his nail. "I stuck her in goal, which she wasn't happy about, but I was six years older than her and she tended to do whatever I wanted. We played for a while, and then she started complaining she was wheezy. Now, I recognize she'd had signs of asthma for a while. She had a recurrent cough. After playing sports and in the cold weather she'd sometimes complain of shortness of breath, but it always went away after a while. One doctor prescribed her an inhaler, but she didn't like using it as none of us really understood asthma, and we didn't realize how important it was. In a family of four kids, nobody has much sympathy with illness."

In spite of his attempt at humor, to his surprise Erin reached out and held his hand, so she'd obviously spotted that this was still difficult. "Go on," she said.

He shivered as she brushed her thumb across the back of his hand. "Eventually Pippa stopped playing," he said distantly, "and sat on the grass. I teased her for a moment, then realized she was really in trouble. I carried her inside but by then she was barely breathing. I rang for an ambulance but she died before it turned up."

Erin pressed her fingers to her mouth. "Oh, Brock. That's awful."

He didn't say anything for a moment, and neither did she. Her hand was warm on his, and he concentrated on the feelings that gentle stroking of his skin aroused in him. He'd been too long without human touch, he thought. He hugged his mother, occasionally kissed a female friend on the cheek, but this was different. It felt intimate and sensual, and it stirred up a confusing swirl of emotions, from guilt to comfort to pleasure.

He swallowed and tried to concentrate. "I'd not been great at school before that—I was bright but messed around a lot, and my grades were all over the place. After she died, though, I decided I was going to become a doctor and do my best to make sure others didn't have to go through what I went through. I want to raise awareness of asthma, and make treatments easier and more readily available for everyone, and to try to take away the fear of medical equipment for kids."

"It was a great idea," Erin said softly, "and you've made such a difference to a huge number of people."

"Well, it'll never bring Pippa back, but it's better than doing nothing."

"It's a lot better than doing nothing."

They smiled at each other. Brock knew she was about to pull her hand away, and he turned his over to hold hers so she couldn't remove it. He ran his thumb over her knuckles. Strange how such an innocent gesture made him feel as if they were the only two people in the room.

Erin looked down at their hands, but she didn't pull away. "So tell me about yourself," she said. "I only know that you're a doctor."

"Well, I can cook, a bit. I'd do more but it's time, you know? I play the guitar, nothing fancy, just strum along to songs and irritate everyone." He grinned. "I like comedies too, and I love a good drama series. I read to relax, thrillers and crime mostly, books that don't take too much brain power. I used to play football and rugby, but don't have the time to commit to a team now, so mainly I just run to keep fit."

"You sound very committed to your work." Erin smiled. "I do admire that. Is it the main reason you're still single?"

He brushed her knuckles again. "Kind of. There's not been much time or opportunity to meet anyone else. But I've not been looking either. Two years sounds a long time but it doesn't feel like it. When

Fleur was dying, I told her I'd never look at another woman again. She just laughed, but I meant every word. Now though…" He paused and then gave a long sigh.

"I know what you mean," Erin said. "It's not quite the same for me, obviously, but when Jack left, I decided I was done with men. I'd had the hassles of pregnancy, then all the issues of a newborn, then the complications of a toddler. It's been hard doing it on my own, but I've managed, and I've told myself I don't need a man. I haven't had time to devote to another person anyway. But sometimes…" Her voice trailed off.

Brock's eyes met hers as she looked up at him, and then his gaze slid to her mouth. He'd not had feelings for a woman for so long, and yet even before he'd met Erin, he'd felt a connection with her he couldn't explain.

It was so complicated. He didn't know if he'd ever get rid of his guilt about betraying Fleur. She'd told him she didn't want him to stay single for the rest of his life, but he'd promised her he'd never love again. What kind of man would it make him if he broke that promise?

And yet in another way it was so simple. He liked Erin. She was gorgeous and he wanted to lean across the table and kiss her, but it was also more than that. It was nice just to talk to someone about something other than work. To have a woman look at him with warmth in her eyes.

For God's sake, he scolded himself, he didn't have to ask her to marry him. And asking her out on a date didn't mean he'd stopped loving or missing his wife. Only that time had moved on, and although a piece of him had died along with Fleur, he was ready for something—or someone—to bring him back to life again.

One step at a time, Brock. No need to rush.

"Next weekend," he said, "providing Ryan's well enough for you to leave… I wondered if you'd like to go away somewhere with me for your birthday. A nice hotel in the Bay, maybe, for a treat after all the stress you've had."

Erin stared at him. Her eyes widened to saucers and she leaned back in her chair, withdrawing her hand from his grip.

Suddenly, he realized how his offer might have sounded. "Oh, I meant separate rooms," he added hastily. "Christ, I'm not that forward."

Her lips curved up, but her face flushed a beautiful shade of pink.

Brock ran a hand through his hair. "I'm making a real hash of this. Can you tell I haven't asked a girl out for about ten years?"

"A little, yeah."

He sighed. *Best to be honest now you've nearly screwed it up, dude.* "I'm sorry. I should have just asked you to dinner. But seriously, I thought it would be a nice gift for you. A night in a hotel with a room to yourself. We could have dinner in the restaurant—a fancy steak or whatever you wanted, a glass of red wine, and a Lagavulin to finish the night off. And then imagine it—a night in a Queen bed on your own, without a small person playing starfish beside you. You could have a decent bath without being interrupted and watch a real movie on the TV without having to turn over for cartoons. And you could drink the whole contents of the mini bar without having to worry about being there for Ryan."

Erin was smiling warmly by now. "Actually that sounds like heaven."

His heart swelled. "Is that a yes?"

She gave a noncommittal shrug. "It's a maybe. It's a lovely gesture, Brock. And you're right—we've been communicating for a long time, but ultimately I don't know you very well. It feels odd accepting such a generous gift from a man."

He reached out and took her hand again, and this time she didn't pull away. "I'm really sorry, I honestly didn't mean it to come out the way it did. I just want to spend some time with you and get to know you a little better, and you've obviously been through a lot lately. You deserve a special treat. I sincerely meant separate rooms, I swear."

"I believe you," she said softly.

"The We Three Kings Foundation often helps out toward accommodation costs for parents, as usually only one person can stay in hospital with the child. We can say we'll pay for your room out of that fund if it makes you feel better."

An impish smile crossed her face. "The fund pays for glasses of Lagavulin, does it?"

He grinned. "No, you'd have to let me pay for that."

She looked down at where he was brushing his thumb across her knuckles. "May I think about it and see how Ryan is toward the end of the week?"

"Of course. I'll book the rooms anyway, but if you decide you'd rather stay with Ryan or you feel too uncomfortable, maybe we can just do lunch at a nearby cafe or something instead."

She nodded. "Okay." Clearing her throat, she pushed back her chair. "I'd better get back upstairs."

"Of course. I'll come with you and pick up my bags."

He accompanied her up the stairs, pausing when they reached the room where he'd changed. "I'll give you a call toward the end of the week, if I don't speak to you before," he said.

"Okay."

He wasn't quite sure what emotion was in her eyes—excitement? Wariness? Amusement? Her lips curved, though, so he knew it was nothing bad.

They were only inches apart, close enough for him to smell her light, flowery perfume and to see the freckles across her nose. Her lips looked soft, and he wanted to kiss her, to dip his tongue into her mouth and see if she tasted as sweet as he suspected. To pull her against him, slide his hands under her T-shirt, and feel her warm skin.

Smiling, he bent his head and touched his lips to her cheek. "Goodbye, Erin."

"Bye." She blushed and walked away, giving him a quick glance over her shoulder before she disappeared into the ward.

Brock grinned and picked up his bags, then headed for the stairs. Georgia was waiting there, and she raised her eyebrows as he walked up.

"Did you pull?" she asked.

He tipped his head to the side and gave her an exasperated look. "Subtle, Miss Banks."

"You don't pay me for subtlety," she said as they walked down the stairs.

He laughed. "Thanks for organizing this. I know you were hoping to see Matt." He winked at her. He had a special fondness for the young woman who worked so hard for sick children. An absolute beauty, Georgia Banks had a troubled past, and he wasn't at all surprised she wasn't interested in his brother. He waited for her to say so.

Sure enough, she said, "Not at all," but to his surprise, her cheeks turned a rosy pink.

He smirked. He'd made two women blush in the space of two minutes. That wasn't bad going.

He opened his mouth to query her further, but they'd reached the bottom of the stairs and Georgia was clearly not going to let herself be questioned. "See you later," she said, and walked away to her car.

Brock hefted his bag over his shoulder and tucked the bag with Dixon's costume under his arm, heading out to the taxi Georgia had arranged to take him to the airport. Someone was playing Christmas carols in their car, and he chuckled when he heard the song We Three Kings.

Humming along, happier than he had been in a long while, he got into the taxi and sat back to daydream as the car drove away.

Chapter Six

"So your father and I were wondering if you'd like to go out for a meal on Saturday for your birthday?"

It was Wednesday lunchtime. Ryan had been released from hospital on the Monday, and after a couple of days' rest, like most kids he'd bounced back as if there had never been anything wrong with him. Erin had been keeping a close eye on him, but he seemed fine.

She was in the middle of making him a sandwich. She'd buttered two slices of bread and was halfway through opening a tin of tuna. Her hand gave an involuntary twitch, and the tin slipped out of the opener and clattered onto the breakfast bar.

"Oops." She picked it up again and carried on, attempting nonchalance. "Um, I'm not sure what I'm doing yet, but thanks. Can I let you know?"

"Of course." Karen Bloom sat on the stool opposite her. Erin knew her mother hated doing nothing and was itching to take over and make the sandwich for her, but to her credit she remained still and didn't comment on the fact that water had leaked from the spilled tin all over the counter. "Are you thinking of going out with your friends? I can babysit if you like."

"I… um…" Erin had always been unable to lie to her mother. Lying to her teachers, her friends, her partners, even her father, had been easy, but there was something in her mother's eye that made her feel as if Karen saw right through her to the fourteen-year-old girl inside.

"Okay, out with it." Karen gave in to her instincts and rose to get a piece of kitchen towel to mop up the spill. "Are you having a party or something?"

"I haven't had a birthday party since I was eleven, Mum."

"And I still can't believe you wanted to wear a Spider-man outfit and not that beautiful princess dress I made for you."

Erin chuckled. "I stood out a bit, didn't I?"

"You did rather. So? What's the plan?"

Concentrating hard, Erin tipped the tuna into a bowl, added mayonnaise, and gave it a stir. "I've... um... had an... um... offer. Sort of."

"An offer? Of what?"

Possibly hot sex with a gorgeous man if I play my cards right.

She cleared her throat. "Brock's asked me out to dinner."

Karen's eyes widened. "Dixon the Dog?"

Erin glanced over her shoulder to where Ryan sat on the floor, playing with his Lego and watching his favorite Disney movie for the hundredth time. He showed no sign of having heard her. The Dixon the Dog plush toy that Brock had given him sat by his side as if also watching the movie. It had been permanently attached to Ryan's hand since his birthday.

Hiding a smile, she brought her gaze back to her mother. "Yes. Although he probably won't be wearing the dog suit."

Karen gave her a wry look. "Well, that's nice. Where does he want to take you?"

Erin tried very hard not to give a rude answer to that one. "That's the thing. He's offered to pay for a night away in a hotel."

Silence fell like early morning mist. Erin spread the tuna mayo on one slice of bread, topped it with a cheese square out of a packet, and put the other slice of bread on top.

"You shouldn't give him that plastic cheese," Karen said. "I bet it has a thousand E numbers in it."

"Ryan likes it. He doesn't like real cheese." She cut the sandwich in half with more force than was necessary, making the tuna squeeze out of the sides onto the counter.

"Or real meat," Karen said, referring to the fact that her grandson would eat chicken nuggets but not chicken, meatballs but not beef, loved sausages but wouldn't go near a slice of pork, and only ate fish if it had fingers.

Erin paused, counted to ten, and placed the sandwiches on a plate with a packet of chips. Her parents had been invaluable after Jack had left her. Karen had come to all her ante-natal classes, she'd been at the birth, and she never said no if Erin asked her to babysit. Although Erin lived in a tiny house and barely had two cents to rub together, her father, Pete, made sure they never went hungry, and that Ryan always had enough clothes and toys so Erin didn't feel a complete failure as a mother. She couldn't have coped without them, and she was incredibly thankful they only lived ten minutes up the road and were willing and able to help out.

Still, it didn't mean they never made her want to pull her hair out. She managed her money as well as she could, but occasionally she gave in and treated herself to something—a pretty scarf in the sale, a sparkly crystal to hang in the window, a pot of flowers for the table—things that, to her, made life worth living. Her father worked in a bank, and he'd pointed out more than once that these things weren't necessities, and until she got herself a proper job and earned enough to clear the bills, she shouldn't waste her money on frivolities. At the ripe old age of twenty-six, she wanted to tell him to stick his advice where the sun didn't shine, but he meant well, he was her father, and she knew he had no real understanding of how hard it was for her to get through the days sometimes, so she let it slide.

With her mother, it was slightly different. Karen had brought up her three children on very little money, and often said how tough it had been, so Erin knew she understood not just not having money to buy stuff, but also not being able to pay for a nanny or kindergarten. Now Ryan had turned three, Erin was officially able to place him at a kindergarten for twenty hours a week for free, but that depended on vacancies, and at the moment the kindie nearest to her had no places until the following February when the oldest children would start primary school.

She knew she had it no harder than the majority of single mums across the world. She had only the one child, and she had both her parents around to help out—not every woman was that lucky. But there were times she felt her mother could have made her life easier. Karen had no problem with pointing out areas where she thought Erin could do better, whether it because she thought her daughter had waited too long to toilet train Ryan, when it was connected to her grandson's eating habits, or when she felt Erin could have been stricter with his behavior. Again, she meant well, and her protectiveness was entirely due to the fact that Erin had struggled to cope when Jack had abandoned her. But even so, it didn't make life easy.

"What hotel?" Karen said eventually, curiosity getting the better of her disapproval.

"I don't know. Somewhere in the Bay, he said."

"He owns Three Wise Men, doesn't he? He must have a few dollars to his name."

"Well, he owns it with his brothers, but yeah, I'm guessing he's not hard up." Erin took the plate into the living room and gave it to her son.

"Dinosaur's starving," Ryan said, and let the T-rex he'd built take a bite out of the tuna sandwich.

"That's cool. One bite for him, one for you." Erin walked back into the kitchen.

Karen frowned. "You shouldn't let him play with his food."

"Mum…" Erin fought the urge to bang her head on the counter and threw the tin into the sink with a clatter. "Aren't you supposed to be somewhere?"

Karen waved her hand. "It won't matter if I'm a few minutes late. What have you said to Brock?"

"I told him I'd let him know."

Her mother raised an eyebrow. "You know he only wants one thing, Erin. And a man with money knows how to get it."

"Mum!"

"I'm telling it like it is, that's all."

"You were the one who encouraged him on the phone! You told him what to buy Ryan."

"Buying a sick child a birthday present is one thing. Proposing an affair is another. I know what you're like—a man flashes a smile at you and everything goes out of the window. You need to keep your wits about you with this one."

Erin bit her lip hard, then blew out a breath. "I admit I didn't see through Jack until it was too late, but one incident doesn't make a trend."

"Oh sweetheart, come on, Jack was hardly the only one. You have terrible taste in men."

Opening her mouth to protest, Erin thought about it, then slowly closed her mouth. She wanted to yell at her mother, but Karen spoke the truth. Erin's first boyfriend had cheated on her with her then best friend. Her second boyfriend broke up with her the day before Valentine's Day. The third had seemed to prefer spending time with his mates to being with her, and when she'd tentatively suggested they see more of each other, he'd dumped her for being too possessive. Ironically, the fourth had wanted to be with her every minute of the day and had been jealous to the point that he'd scared her, flying off the handle whenever he caught her even exchanging the time of day with another man.

The fifth had been Jack. Karen was right—she had a terrible taste in men, and the realization brought angry tears rushing to Erin's eyes.

Karen sighed. "Oh, honey…" Hastily, she walked around the breakfast bar and enfolded her daughter in her arms.

Erin gritted her teeth. Karen's arms were warm, her hand gentle as it stroked her arm. Her mother always had to pick up the pieces after each disastrous relationship ended. It wasn't surprising she was wary for her daughter.

"Surely statistically I'm due to meet someone nice?" Erin sniffed.

"You'd think." Karen went over to switch the kettle on.

"He's really nice, mum," Erin said softly, thinking of Brock's smile, and his gentle concern on the phone.

"I'm sure he is. And I suppose he'd be able to provide well for you and Ryan."

Erin stiffened. "That's not why I'm thinking about going out with him."

"It's nothing to be ashamed of, love. It's animal instinct, isn't it? Choosing the best mate we can find who we think will care for our young."

"Even so. I'm not interested in his money."

"So you're paying for this hotel, are you?"

Erin locked gazes with her mother. "I'm not allowed presents on my birthday now?"

"A bunch of red roses is a gift. So is a box of chocolates. You've just met the man. You're really saying you'll let him pay for a night away in a hotel. What's he going to do, book two rooms?" Karen laughed.

Erin's cheeks warmed. "That's exactly what he's doing."

"Oh, sweetheart, come on," Karen scoffed. "You are so incredibly naive. You're twenty-six, not sixteen."

Erin glared at her. "Don't you think it's possible for someone to be altruistic in this day and age? To give a gift without wanting something in return?"

Karen folded her arms. "No."

"Then I pity you," Erin said harshly. "What a terrible world you must live in."

"I live in the real world. And I'm not the single mother struggling to make ends meet because her idiot boyfriend wouldn't recognize his child."

That really hurt. Erin inhaled and swallowed hard. "Ouch."

Immediately, regret crossed Karen's face. "I'm sorry. I shouldn't have said that. Damn it, I always go too far. I only want what's best for you, my love."

"I know."

"I just don't want you to get hurt again."

"I know."

"Just be careful. It's possible this man is being unselfish. Maybe he genuinely wants to be nice. But money is a strange thing—it's like mistletoe. It's attractive, but it's parasitic—it drains all the good things out of you. I'm not saying he doesn't like the look of you, but once he sees your lifestyle, he'll think you're after his money. It'll eat at him, the same way it will eat at you every time you wonder whether you're only with him because of it, and don't look at me like that. I know you, and I know how your brain works."

"I think I've had about as much honesty as I can take today." Erin got her mother's handbag and held it out to her. "You'd better go or you'll be late."

Karen looked suddenly distressed. Although she was often outspoken, the two of them rarely argued. "I'm sorry."

"It's okay. You're probably right. I just need to think about it."

Reluctantly, Karen kissed her on the cheek, then went and kissed Ryan goodbye before following her daughter to the door. "I really am sorry," she said when they reached it. "I'm so worried about you getting hurt again, that's all."

"I know, Mum. Don't worry, it's all good. I'll see you tomorrow—are you still okay to babysit for Ryan while I go and visit Caitlin?" Erin was due to meet her old school friend up in Mangonui for the afternoon. They'd arranged it ages ago, and although she was reluctant to leave Ryan after he'd been unwell, he was so full of spirits now that she felt able to leave him with her parents for an afternoon.

"Of course. I'll see you around eleven?"

"Sure. Bye."

Erin closed the door behind her mother, and went and sat on the sofa.

Ryan had finished his sandwich, and he got up, came over to her, and climbed onto her lap. "I'm still hungry," he announced. "Can I have a biscuit?"

"I think we should have a walk down to the shop and buy a huge bar of chocolate," Erin said, knowing that would annoy both of her parents.

Her son's eyes lit up. "Milky Bar?"

"Absolutely. We'll get two bars. Milky Bar for you and Dairy Milk for me."

He flung his arms around her and planted a wet kiss on her cheek. "Can Dixon come?"

She hugged him back, fighting tears once again. "Of course. Does he like chocolate?"

Ryan thought about it. "He likes Smarties."

Erin laughed. "Then we'll get some Smarties as well." The money in her purse was put aside for the week's shopping, but screw it. She would spend a couple of dollars of it on chocolate and eat beans on toast for a week if it meant making Ryan's eyes light up like that for once.

She closed her eyes and buried her face in Ryan's soft neck. Her mother was right—if she met someone with money, she'd never have to scrimp and save again, but she'd never be able to stop herself wondering if that was why she was with him. Whenever they argued, he'd always be able to throw it in her face, and it would turn things sour very quickly.

As much as she hated to admit it, it was probably best that she didn't go away with him. She'd text him later and say no.

Chapter Seven

"He said what?"

Caitlin's voice was loud enough to cut across the cafe, and Erin winced as the other customers glanced over at them with amusement.

It was Thursday, and they were catching up in Caitlin's Treats to Tempt You chocolate, coffee, and ice cream shop in Mangonui. Erin had gone to school with Caitlin, and she'd missed Cait and her sister Elle a lot after they'd moved from Whangarei eighty or so miles away to Doubtless Bay. It was easier now Erin lived in Kerikeri and it only took forty-five minutes to drive.

"Sorry." Caitlin pulled an *eek* face. "You shocked me."

"Imagine how I felt. A night away in a hotel! It's like something out of a movie." Erin carved out another scoop of the sumptuous Christmas pudding ice cream Caitlin had dished up. She'd debated long and hard whether to tell Caitlin about Brock. She'd spent all of Wednesday evening with her phone in her hand, trying to text him to tell him she wouldn't be going at the weekend, but for some reason her fingers had refused to type the message. In the end, she'd decided she'd tell Caitlin about him, and if Cait agreed with her mother that it was a terrible idea, she'd text him there and then.

And if Cait disagreed... Erin had spent most of the night dreaming about what that would mean.

"Seriously," she said, "what was I supposed to say to that?"

"How about 'excuse me while I bite your hand off?'" Caitlin laughed and sipped her latte, then stared at her friend. "Wait, don't tell me you said no?"

"I said maybe. That I'd let him know toward the end of the week." Erin sighed and sucked the ice cream off the spoon. "I don't know what to say, to be honest."

Caitlin drew her brows together as if Erin had said she'd refused a free truck load of chocolate. "I don't understand. You're not making sense, woman. He's gorgeous, right?"

Erin thought about the muscular chest she'd caught a glimpse of. "Mmm. Dreamy as."

"And he's as rich as Rockefeller's richest uncle." It was a statement, not a question.

"I have no idea."

Caitlin rolled her eyes. "Jeez. Didn't you read the article in the Herald?"

"No, I missed it. I meant to look it up but I forgot."

"Erin, the King family was wealthy to start with, but the three brothers have made an absolute fortune. For God's sake, they give more to charity each week than I'll make in my lifetime. They're billionaires, all three of them."

Erin didn't know a person could choke on ice cream. She grabbed a serviette and covered her mouth as she struggled to catch her breath. "What?" she said when she was finally able to speak.

Caitlin raised an eyebrow. "Now tell me you're going to say no."

Her jaw dropping, Erin tried to process this new information. Brock was a billionaire? Oh dear God. She'd had no idea. She'd known he ran the Three Wise Men with his brothers, and she'd guessed he wasn't exactly hard up. But a billionaire... Erin couldn't even conceive of how much money that was.

Across the table, Caitlin started to giggle at her expression.

"Stop it." Erin put her face in her hands, thinking of her mother. "Oh... what am I going to do?"

"Seriously? I don't understand the problem."

"I can't go out with him, Cait, he'll think I'm just after his money."

"But you didn't even know he had any until now."

"Well, I knew he had money, although I didn't know how much. But he doesn't know that."

Caitlin sighed. "Oh give the guy a break. Okay so he doesn't have to worry about where the next meal is coming from—does that mean he doesn't want to date anymore?"

"Don't you think it's weird though? I'd only just met the man and he offered to take me away for the night."

"But you said you believed him when he told you he meant separate bedrooms."

"I did. That's not the point."

"What is the point?"

"I don't know." Erin couldn't seem to vocalize her angst. "Mum said—"

"Argh!" Caitlin stuck her fingers in her ears. "No. Talk. About. Mothers. Please don't tell me you're making a decision based on Karen's advice."

"She put doubts in my mind. And since then I've found it difficult to believe he's genuine."

Caitlin's expression softened. "Just because Jack was a bastard doesn't mean all men are the same. Not everyone is out for themselves. Sometimes people genuinely want to help."

It was almost exactly what Erin had said to her mother but, wanting reassurance, she just said, "Really?"

"He came all the way from Auckland to give your son a birthday present and to meet you because he liked the sound of you on the phone. That doesn't sound selfish to me."

"I suppose. So you don't think he'll expect anything from me in return for treating me to a night away? He's not going to expect me to go back to his room?"

An impish light filled Caitlin's eyes. "Would it be a problem if he did?"

"Cait!"

"Well. How long has it been since you've had sex?"

"Uh… Let's just say it's been a while."

For the past three years, life had consisted of high chairs, Disney movies, toddler groups, and doctor's visits. Erin couldn't remember the last time she'd worn a skirt, let alone anything that had any shape to it. She wore her hair permanently in a ponytail and never painted her fingernails. She'd been a mum for so long, she'd forgotten how to be a woman.

"I'm not sure I even remember how to do it," she said.

Caitlin grinned. "I bet he has a few techniques up his sleeve to help you remember. Don't you think a one-night stand would be fun?"

"Oh my God, I couldn't."

"Why?"

"I don't know… Stretch marks? Baby tummy?"

"You're not fifteen, Erin. He won't expect you to have a fifteen-year-old's body."

"Yeah but…" Desperation mingled with a growing excitement. She couldn't possibly have a one-night stand with Brock King. Could she? Of course she couldn't.

Panic overrode the excitement. "I couldn't, Cait. It's been so long. And he'd expect all sorts of things."

"Like what?" Caitlin said with amusement.

"I don't know. Fancy stuff."

"Clowns outfits and trapeze work?"

"Don't make fun of me. You know what I mean. Special techniques and… stuff."

Caitlin laughed. "Sweetie, you're gorgeous, you're sexy beneath all the angst, and you're willing. That's all a guy needs, believe me."

"What's all a guy needs?" The male voice made them both jump. Erin hadn't seen him walk up. It was Caitlin's fiancé, the sexy chef who ran the restaurant a few doors down from the chocolate shop.

"Hey, Fox." Erin smiled as he bent to kiss her on the cheek.

"Hey." He pulled up a chair, turned it around and straddled it.

"Go away," Caitlin said. "We're having a private conversation."

"What's all a guy needs?" he asked, ignoring her. He raised his eyebrows at Erin. "Are you dating?"

Erin blushed. "No. Yes. Maybe."

Fox grinned. "Who is he?"

"He's a gorgeous billionaire," Caitlin said. "By the way we're breaking up so I can date his brother."

"Yeah, right." Fox caught her long blonde braid and pulled her toward him for a kiss.

"Ow." She glared at him, then gave in and kissed him back. Afterward, she tried to push him away, but he refused to let her go, and the kiss turned into a long smooch.

"Oh, get a room you two." Erin rolled her eyes and stuck her spoon back in her ice cream.

Fox let her go and laughed. "So, a billionaire?"

"He wants to take her away for a dirty weekend," Caitlin said.

Erin closed her eyes. "Cait…"

"I hope you said yes." Fox stuck Cait's spoon in Erin's ice cream and stole a spoonful.

"She's thinking of saying no," Cait advised.

Fox raised an eyebrow. "I hope you took her temperature because she's clearly coming down with something."

"That's what I said. She'd be bonkers not to go."

Erin sighed. "He's a great guy, a doctor who I've spoken to lots of time on the forums. He came all the way from Auckland for Ryan's birthday, and he's offered to pay for one night in a hotel for me for my birthday on Saturday. I'm just worried about what he'd expect in return. He told me he'll book two rooms but... well. Do you think it's possible for a man to be truly altruistic?"

Fox took another spoonful of ice cream and gave her an amused look. "You're asking me if it's possible he's arranged this out of the goodness of his heart?"

"Yes." She knew her voice expressed her doubt.

He considered her as he sucked the ice cream off the spoon. His eyes had a hint of steel about them. "You're asking me, a guy, whether it's possible that another man might, for once, want to do something nice for you without having an ulterior motive. You don't have a very high opinion of our gender, do you?"

Caitlin smacked his wrist. "Don't embarrass her. You never met Jack. He was a dick. Sorry, Erin, I know he's the father of your child, but he was."

"I'm not arguing with you," Erin said wryly.

"Look," Fox said. "Let's assume this new guy isn't a dick, and he's actually one of the good guys. Let's assume it was me, and I was in his position, and I met this girl who lived a few hours away that I really liked. I'm a billionaire so money isn't an issue."

"I like this fantasy," Caitlin said.

He grinned but carried on. "I want to get to know this girl better, and it's her birthday, and her son's just been in hospital, so I decide to treat her to a night away in a hotel. I book myself in the same place because I live three hours away and I want to take her to dinner and have a drink with her, but I book a separate room because I'm a nice guy and I'd never assume a woman would just go to bed with me."

Caitlin snorted. This time he didn't smile but raised his eyebrow at her. She bit her lip and lowered her eyes. Erin hid a smile. Fox Wilde was the only man who'd ever been able to tame the inimitable Caitlin.

"I like her," he said. "I want to treat her. Get to know her. I might secretly hope that things will develop, and if they do, then we're in the right sort of place where we can take it further if we both feel like it. But I wouldn't expect it. And I think it's a real shame a guy can't treat a girl without her suspecting he has ulterior motives."

Erin studied her ice cream bowl. "Sorry," she said in a small voice. "I didn't mean to sound insulting."

He sighed. "Like I said, I'm sure he won't be disappointed if things develop, but if this is a first date I'm sure he's not expecting anything. I don't see why you shouldn't go and have fun. Go to dinner with the guy. Get to know him. Have a drink. Enjoy yourself. And if you like him…" He shrugged and a smile curved his lips. "See where it leads."

"Wouldn't he think I was a slut if I went back to his room?"

That made Fox laugh. He rose from the chair and leaned over to kiss her forehead. "He'd think he was the luckiest man on earth, I'm sure. This is the twenty-first century, Erin. I don't think you'll be shunned from society if you're seen alone without a chaperone." He winked at his fiancée. "See you later."

"See ya." Caitlin watched him go, then turned amused eyes back to her friend. "Did that help?"

"I insulted him," Erin said. "I didn't mean to. Sorry."

"Of course you didn't. He would have been angry that guys like Jack give men a bad name and make us not trust the good ones. We joke about it, but let's face it, none of the guys I know would take advantage of a girl."

Erin thought about the men married to Caitlin's friends up in Mangonui whom she'd met on a few occasions: Kole, Joss, Stuart, and Owen, all of whom were good, decent guys. "I suppose Fox is right. Hoping is different to expecting."

"Of course it is. It's annoying, but he's usually right. Look, you'd be daft not to go. Forget about Brock being rich."

"That's easier said than done."

"I appreciate that. What I mean is, try not to let that influence the way you think about him. If anything, it probably means he's more generous than your ordinary guy. He wouldn't think twice about giving a gift that other men might falter at. A night in a hotel will be peanuts to him. What hotel is it, anyway?"

"He didn't say. I'm guessing it's not going to be a cheap B&B."

"Yeah. But my point is that it wouldn't even enter his head that a gift like that would make you feel uncomfortable. It'll embarrass him more if you say no."

"I suppose." Excitement rose inside her. "Am I really going to do this? Go away for a night with a man?"

"You are. You'd better get your legs waxed."

"Cait!"

"And your bikini line."

"Oh my God."

Caitlin giggled. "I hope you have fun. And look, if you feel too awkward about taking things further, just thank him for a lovely meal and go back to your room. It doesn't mean you can't see him again. I'm sure he'll be expecting you to take it slow. He knows you're a single mum and that it's been a while since you went out with anyone. He sounds like a nice guy, Erin. Why don't you treat him like one?"

"Yeah. In a way I feel ashamed for having such low expectations." Anger surged through her. That's what Jack had done to her. He'd ruined her for every other guy because he'd been such a complete and utter bastard. "I don't know why I ever liked him. I can't believe I went out with him."

Caitlin had obviously kept up with Erin's change of tack. "You trusted him—and why wouldn't you? The majority of men are nice. The majority of the human race is nice. But there is a small percentage that isn't, and they spoil it for everyone else, destroying our trust. It's Christmas though. Isn't it a time for miracles? Maybe this is the guy you're supposed to be with. Maybe this is Mr. Right."

"Maybe," Erin said doubtfully, "let's not jump to conclusions. I don't want to get my hopes up."

Caitlin reached out and rubbed Erin's arm. "Jack really did a number on you, didn't he?"

Erin knew she didn't have to explain how hard it had been when her ex had shown his true colors. She'd spoken to Cait a lot on the phone at the time, so Cait was perfectly aware how difficult it had been.

"Don't let him spoil this thing—whatever it ends up being—with Brock," Cait said. "I know you doubt your own instincts now, but try to trust them at the weekend. Go with your gut feeling, and believe in the magic of Christmas."

"I'll try." Erin finished off her ice cream. It wouldn't be easy to get rid of all her doubts. Jack had destroyed her trust, and it seemed impossible to get it back. Could Brock really be as nice as he seemed?

Chapter Eight

Brock glanced across at Erin. She sat beside him in his car, looking out of the window at the countryside flashing by. True, it was a splendid view, the hills an emerald green in the summer sun, the sea glittering on either side of them as they headed along the peninsula to Opito Bay. But even though it was magnificent, it didn't explain why she wasn't saying anything.

It had taken until Thursday for her to accept his invitation to go away for the night. He'd texted on Monday to ask how Ryan was doing, and she'd replied to tell him he'd finally been discharged from hospital. After that, over the next few days, they'd exchanged several chatty, light-hearted texts a day, mostly about Ryan, sometimes about what they were up to and how their day was going. He'd fought against his urge to ask if she'd made up her mind, knowing he had to let her come to her own decision without seeming to pressure her, and he'd been relieved when she'd finally sent the text on Thursday.

I've decided, by the way. The answer's yes.

His heart had leapt like a sixteen-year-old boy's after he'd asked a girl to go to the school ball. *Excellent*, he'd replied, a big grin on his face, *shall I pick you up on Saturday at one o'clock?*

I look forward to it, she'd said.

They hadn't mentioned it again, although they'd continued to exchange texts. He'd grown used to his mobile vibrating in his pocket. He liked holding appointments with the delicious anticipation of knowing he had another message to read from her, and he didn't miss the glow it gave him every time he saw her name on the screen.

He'd arrived at Erin's house on Saturday shortly before one to find her ready and waiting with her bag packed. Her eyes had been bright with excitement, and she'd even given him a quick kiss on the cheek before she'd gotten into the car. He'd wondered whether she'd find it difficult to leave her son, but the boy had waved goodbye to her at the door, holding his grandma's hand, and she'd seemed happy enough when they'd driven away.

Over the last ten minutes, though, she'd grown quiet, and Brock had the feeling she was regretting her decision to go with him.

As he glanced over at her again, he saw that her brow had furrowed.

"I thought we were heading to Sandcombe," she said, referring to the small but pleasant hotel nestled in the bush overlooking the marina. He'd just passed the turnoff for it. "Where are we going?"

"Paua Cliffs," he said.

Erin's eyes widened. "Oh my God, seriously?"

He gave her an amused glance. "Have you been there?"

"Of course I haven't been there. A room costs more than a month's rent! Are we really going there?"

"You want me to turn around? I can get a room for ninety bucks at the motel on the main road if you'd rather." He was joking, but as he saw the look on her face, he realized Matt had been right.

The day after he'd met Erin at the hospital, he'd told his brothers what he'd organized for the following weekend. Charlie hadn't seen anything wrong with what he'd done, but then Charlie knew more about his laboratory than he knew about women, whereas Matt was more attuned to the female species than both his brothers put together.

"You fucking idiot," Matt had said. "We finally get you to go out with someone and you want to take her to a hotel. She's going to wonder what you want in return."

"I don't want anything in return," Brock had said, puzzled. "It's a gift. It's her birthday."

"Dude, even men who've known their wives for thirty years only buy them an ironing board for their birthday. No wonder the poor girl's concerned. It looks as if you're taking her away for a dirty weekend."

"I..." Brock had remembered the look on her face when he'd first mentioned it. "But I told her I'd book two rooms."

"So sex didn't enter your head at all then?"

"Well I wouldn't go that far. But I swear that's not why I suggested it. I thought I'd take her to Paua Cliffs. I thought she'd enjoy it—a nice dinner and then a room to herself. Women like that."

"Aah," Charlie had said, "Paua Cliffs. Nice. Classy."

"Yeah. She'll definitely think you want sex if you take her there," Matt had advised. "You should have gotten her a box of chocolates and a dozen roses."

"She's a single mum. She doesn't want flowers scattering petals over all the Lego on the carpet, more mess to clear up. What she wants is time to herself."

"With you knocking on the door asking for a cup of sugar halfway through the night?"

Brock had sworn at his brother and hung up. Sometimes he felt as if they were all still teenagers.

Now, though, he had to acknowledge that, as usual, his brother had been right, and he should have stuck to chocolates and flowers.

Seeing a picnic stop ahead, he signaled and pulled over, then turned off the engine. A family sat at a table further along, munching on their sandwiches as they looked over the bay, but Brock ignored them, unclipped his seatbelt, and turned in the seat to look at Erin.

Her eyes were wide, puzzled. "What's up?" she asked.

"Perhaps we should get something out in the open," he advised. "As a family, the Kings don't struggle to make ends meet."

"I've gathered that."

"All three of us work hard—I can't honestly remember the last time I took a whole weekend off. I save lives on a regular basis—I'm not being flash, it's just a fact, and I give an alarming amount to charity. So I'm not going to apologize for having money, or for wanting to spend a tiny proportion of it on the first beautiful woman I've seen in two years who presses my buttons."

Her lips curved up a little. "I press your buttons?"

He sighed. "You do, Miss Bloom. I hope it's acceptable to say that."

"You're being very generous," she said. "I must sound terribly rude to you."

"Not at all. Matt's already given me a lecture about the appropriateness of asking a woman I barely know to go away with me. I know I've made a faux pas and I'm sorry—if I had my time again I would have just asked you to dinner. Rest assured I meant well, and I just want you to have a nice break and a good time. The thing is, if you've changed your mind, I'd rather you say now. I won't be upset. I can't say I won't be disappointed because I was looking forward to having dinner with you tonight, but I'll understand. But if you decide to come with me, then maybe we can put this behind us, move on, and just have a nice evening." He heard a hint of steel creep into his voice and he stopped talking. He didn't want to spend the rest of the day apologizing for having money or for wanting to treat her on her birthday. Equally, he wanted her to feel comfortable, or what was the point?

He wondered whether she'd be angry at his tone, but to his surprise a small smile played on her lips. "I know you meant well," she murmured. "I'm just a bit nervous."

That surprised him. "Nervous?"

She gave the little sexy shrug he was beginning to adore. "It's been a long time since I've been on a date. I've forgotten the... protocol." She wrinkled her nose.

He smiled. She wore jeans and a white shirt, and she was as fresh and summery as the warm breeze blowing through the open window. "There's no protocol," he told her. "Not with me anyway. I just want you to be yourself. To have a good time." He decided honesty was the best policy. "Look, there's no doubt it's strange for both of us. I haven't dated anyone since Fleur died, and I have to admit I feel odd about it."

Erin's expression softened. "Of course, I'm sorry, I didn't think of that."

"Why would you? I know most people think it's weird to have waited so long before getting back into the dating game. Charlie and Matt have been trying to get me to go out with girls for ages, but I just wasn't ready, I guess."

"Are you ready now?" she asked softly. Her eyes were the color of the ocean behind her, a deep blue. The breeze lifted the strands of hair that had fallen out of her clip, and they fluttered around her face. Outside, the soothing wash of waves and the singing of cicadas were the only sounds to be heard. He felt as if time had paused, and even the birds were listening with bated breath to their conversation.

"Part of me feels disloyal," he admitted. "That people will think I don't love her anymore, and that breaks my heart. But equally, I need something else in my life other than work. I can't tell you how happy I've been over the last few days, waiting for my phone to buzz in my pocket to say you've texted. I've felt like a schoolkid, and it's been good. I've felt alive again, and I want to keep on feeling alive."

"Okay," she whispered. "We'll take it slowly."

"Step by step," he said. "Today, dinner in a nice restaurant to celebrate your birthday. And we'll see how it goes." He meant in the future—whether she'd want to see him again, but the mischievous light in her eyes told him she thought he was talking about what happened after dinner. "Erin," he scolded.

She pressed her lips together, trying not to laugh, but she wasn't able to stop a giggle breaking out. "Your face is a picture," she said.

He shook his head. "You're not the only one who doesn't know the protocol." He hadn't even kissed a girl for over two years, let alone done anything more intimate than that.

Her expression softened again as if she'd read his mind. "It must have been difficult for you, losing your wife. It's bad enough when you're seventy, but when you're only... How old are you?"

"Thirty-one."

"...thirty-one, I can only imagine how hard it must be. Brock, what you said about not expecting anything, it goes both ways. Whatever happens between us, if at any point you feel as if you want to slow down, I want you to say. I don't want to make you feel bad."

He smiled at the sheer lunacy of that statement. "You don't make me feel bad. Quite the opposite."

"I'm glad."

"In fact," he said softly, his gaze dropping to her mouth, "I know it's inappropriate this early on a date, and Matt would kill me if he could hear me, but all I can think about is how much I want to kiss you. Is that terrible?"

Erin moistened her lips with the tip of her tongue. "Well, maybe we should test the water, so to speak. Try it and see how we feel afterward."

"Maybe we should." His heart thundered, but he told himself, *Take it slow.* He waited for a moment as she unclipped her seatbelt, and he inhaled the sweet summer breeze that filtered into the car, bringing with it the smell of the sea and the scent of sun lotion from Erin's skin.

She turned and moved forward a little in her seat, leaning an elbow on the rest between them, and tipped her head to the side as she met his gaze.

Brock moved to meet her, resting one arm on the seat behind her, and lifted the other hand to cup her face. He brushed his thumb across her cheekbone, across the freckles that peppered her lightly-tanned skin, and lowered his mouth, stopping when his lips were a fraction of an inch from hers.

Her breath whispered across his lips as she exhaled. So close, and yet he hadn't kissed her yet. There was still time to stop, to put off this last, final betrayal. If he moved back now, he'd be able to tell himself he'd remained faithful to Fleur. He would have fought his weakness and stayed strong in his grief, encased in the shadows in which he'd hidden for the last two years.

But the day was too beautiful, full of light and life. A couple of huge Red Admiral butterflies fluttered past the window, and a flash of color behind Erin told him a rosella had swooped over the grass. In the distance, the children of the family having lunch at the picnic table laughed as they threw a Frisbee to one another, and someone called out from the boat further down on the water. It was summer, and it was almost Christmas, a time to celebrate the birth of things, not the end.

Erin was waiting patiently, maybe sensing his internal struggle, her gaze gently caressing his face. Her hand came up and she trailed a finger along his eyebrow, removing a strand of hair that the breeze had blown into his eye, and her touch—even though it was innocent and innocuous—was enough to flick a switch inside him.

He let out the breath he'd been holding, a long slow sigh of acceptance.

Erin's lips curved up a little, and then she moved the last fraction of an inch to touch her lips to his.

They were as soft and light as if one of the butterflies had brushed against him, the briefest of kisses, tentative and shy enough to make him melt.

She moved back a little and met his gaze again as if to say, Okay?

Brock felt as if he'd been kissed by summer itself. How could anything as beautiful as that be wrong?

After giving a short, exultant laugh, he slid his hand into her hair, and lowered his lips again.

This time he kissed her, moving his mouth across hers slowly but firmly, closing his eyes and enjoying the sensation of being near to someone again, being intimate. Her hair felt silky in his fingers, her cheeks warming beneath his palm as he continued to kiss her. She murmured low in her throat, a purr of approval, sliding her hand into his hair, and he shivered when she clenched her fingers in the short strands.

It was a brief kiss, hardly a steamy smooch, and yet it was the most erotic thing that had happened to him in years. His blood raced around his body, and his jeans tightened as his erection miraculously sprang to life. He wanted to plunge his tongue into her mouth and deepen the kiss, pull her toward him and slide his hands under her white shirt, but this was only supposed to be a trial, a peck, a testing of the water.

Startled at the speed of his arousal, he lifted his head. His breaths came quickly and, to his surprise, she was breathing fast too. Her eyes fluttered open, and she swallowed, moistened her lips, and said, "Wow."

Chapter Nine

Erin's heart thundered like a set of tracks with the approach of a train. To her relief, Brock appeared to be similarly affected, his pupils dilated and his chest heaving with fast, deep breaths.

"Yeah," he said at her outburst. "Wow."

They both moved back, studying each other cautiously. Erin felt an urge to giggle, but held it in, afraid he was about to tell her he felt too disloyal and he was going to have to take her home.

He didn't though. Instead, he gave a mischievous smile. "That was nice."

"Mmm." *Understatement of the year,* she thought. "It didn't make you feel bad?"

He laughed and looked out of the window, scratching the back of his neck. "No, Erin, it didn't make me feel bad." He turned back to face the wheel, started the engine, then gave her an exasperated, slightly apologetic look as he shifted in the seat and adjusted his jeans. "Sorry."

This time the laughter wouldn't be stopped. She clapped her hand over her mouth, but it burst from her in infectious giggles.

"Yeah, you can laugh," Brock said wryly as he pulled away. "It's unfair that men can't hide their… feelings like women can. And put your seatbelt on."

She clipped it in, still chuckling, feeling a burst of happiness brighter than she'd felt for years. "Thank you so much for this. Even if we were to turn around and go home now, I've had a wonderful time."

He laughed and reached out to take her hand. "Well that's a good start. Let's try to carry that feeling through to tomorrow, eh?"

She smiled and squeezed his fingers, and he squeezed them back before releasing her hand to hold the wheel.

Looking out of the window again, she pressed the button to lower it right down so she could feel the warm summer breeze across her face, and closed her eyes.

"I can put the air con on if you want," he reminded her.

"I prefer having the window open," she said without opening her eyes. "Like a dog. I'd hang my tongue out if I could." She heard him laugh and smiled, breathing in the fresh Kiwi air.

She hadn't expected the kiss. And what a kiss it had been… It had felt as sensual and erotic as if they'd been naked in bed together. Erin shivered at the thought. For the first time, she felt that if the evening ended that way, maybe it wouldn't be such a bad thing after all…

"There it is."

Erin opened her eyes to see a slope leading down to the exclusive Paua Cliffs hotel overlooking the glistening Pacific Ocean. She'd seen a TV feature on it once. They'd said movie stars often had their honeymoons there. She'd never been anywhere like it.

Brock was right though—if she was going through with this, she had to deal with the fact that he was loaded. Even rich guys had to date, and it wasn't his fault that she wasn't used to having money. He could have picked some diamond-studded bimbo to take out, but he hadn't, he'd picked her, and he didn't deserve to have her getting on her high horse every five minutes, acting noble and refusing to accept his generous gift. She had to move on. She'd been given a fantastic opportunity and a wonderful birthday present, and it would be rude to keep bringing up how much he'd spent.

"It's beautiful," she said, meaning it. The white buildings had terracotta-colored roofs that glowed warmly in the sunlight. A huge golf course lay spread out to the west, while to the east the Pacific sparkled like tinsel.

"It's a nice place by all accounts." Brock signaled and took the turnoff, heading down the long drive to the buildings.

"You haven't been here before?"

"No. Never got around to it."

For some reason that pleased her. She had no issues with him having been married before, and she was touched to be the first woman he'd come close to dating. But it was nice to know he hadn't brought his wife here.

The road snaked alongside the golf course and up to the complex of buildings. "What a beautiful day." Erin lowered her sunglasses against the glare of the bright December sun.

"Warmest December for five years apparently." Brock headed the car around the looping drive to the building marked Reception, parked, and turned off the engine. "Let's check in, and then we can head up to our rooms for a look around. Maybe after you've settled in, you'd like to go for a walk down to the beach?"

"That sounds lovely." Erin got out with him, shut the door, and hesitated. "Should I get my bag now?"

"Someone will bring them up to the rooms shortly," he advised with a smile.

Erin had never had someone carry her bags up for her before. Her cheeks warmed. "Oh."

Brock grinned and held out a hand. "You'll soon get used to it. Come on."

She walked forward and took his hand, a tingle descending her spine at the feel of his warm skin on hers. "I should have dressed up a bit, sorry. I didn't think." Not that she looked skanky, but her white shirt and faded jeans had seen better days.

"You look gorgeous," he said as they walked into the foyer. "But it wouldn't matter what you wore. This is New Zealand, remember? There will be guys eating dinner tonight wearing shorts and a T-shirt, I'm telling you."

"Oh, I have a nice dress for dinner," she said as they crossed the elegant tiled floor to the main desk.

Brock raised an eyebrow. "Oh?"

"Mmm." She felt a surge of naughtiness at his sudden interest. "Quite low and revealing. I hope it doesn't put you off your meal."

They stopped at the desk, and for a brief moment she could see she'd completely thrown his concentration. He stared at her, then stared at the receptionist as he struggled to remember what he was doing there. "Um... Ms. Erin Bloom and Dr. Brock King checking in, please."

"Of course sir." The receptionist tapped in their names. "Two luxury rooms with sea views?"

"That's right." Brock slid his credit card across to her and took the paper to sign.

Erin tried not to let her jaw drop. Not only were they staying at Paua Cliffs but they were in luxury rooms. What did that mean? Was everything plated gold? Were there slaves waiting inside to fan her with giant palm leaves?

It wasn't quite that luxurious, but it wasn't far off. A young man dressed in a dark gray uniform collected their bags and took them out of the foyer and across a courtyard to a row of long, low buildings. He stopped outside one and opened it with a key, then stood back to let Erin pass.

She walked into the room, and this time couldn't stop her jaw dropping. It was all open plan, one enormous room, easily as big as her house. The whole front wall was made from glass panels with a magnificent view of the bay. Outside the large glass sliding doors in the center, a generous deck housed a table and chairs and, in the corner, a large hot tub that would easily fit two people.

Trying not to think about climbing into bubbling water with a tall, muscular billionaire, she looked past it to the private, fenced grassy bank leading down to the hotel's sandy beach. The Pacific Ocean beckoned invitingly, the same color as the baby-blue summer sky.

She was half aware of Brock standing in the doorway, leaning against the wall and watching her with a smile while she turned and investigated the room. To the left was a living room area with a cream suite, a TV that must have been at least fifty inches from corner to corner, and a chrome-and-glass table and chairs. The whole floor was made from rich red rimu wood, polished to a high shine. Large green ferns and simple paintings of seascapes on the walls provided an elegant touch of color. There was also a small kitchen far to the left near the table and chairs with all the modern conveniences a woman could need, should she be mad enough to want to cook her own meal and not eat out like most normal people.

To the right, a huge bed faced the view, with white and red pillows and a luxurious white duvet, and surrounded by four posts from which hung gorgeous shimmering drapes to provide privacy— not that it was needed, as nobody would be able to see in from the beach.

She'd have to take loads of photos or Caitlin would never believe her!

The porter disappeared to take Brock's case into the room next door. Brock pushed himself off the doorjamb and walked toward her.

"Do you like it?" His smile told her he'd guessed her answer.

"It's beautiful." Laughter burst from her. What an understatement! Nothing in this place would be missing, chipped, or dirty like in some of the cheap motels she'd stayed in. Everything would be clean, polished, and in perfect working order. "I don't know what to say. It's amazing. It's like somewhere the Queen of England would stay."

He grinned and glanced around. "Yeah, it's pretty fancy." His gaze came back to her, and he tipped his head. "Too fancy?"

Erin took a deep breath. She wasn't going to bring up the subject of money again. "It's wonderful. I'm absolutely thrilled, Brock. Thank you."

Pleasure lit his face. "Okay then." A hint of relief crossed his features—he really had expected her to say she couldn't accept it and leave. "Well, I'll leave you to settle in for a while." He checked his watch. "It's just gone four. Is thirty minutes long enough for a rest? We could go for a walk for an hour or so, then come back and have a little while to get ready for dinner at seven."

"That sounds lovely."

"Right, see you in a bit." He winked at her. "Don't forget, this is your birthday treat. Help yourself to the mini bar or order room service—whatever you want. Make the most of it. But it's a five star restaurant and seafood is their specialty so you want to make sure you're hungry."

"I will." She walked up to him, placed her hands on his chest, and rose onto her tiptoes. "Thank you," she whispered before pressing her lips to his.

His hand rose to cup her head, and the quick peck turned into a longer kiss that sent her heart racing all over again.

"Ooh," she said when he eventually let her go.

"Sorry. Couldn't resist." He smirked and left the room, closing the door behind him.

Erin stared after him for a while, then turned and looked at the room again. Throwing her arms in the air, she laughed and twirled in the center. It was her birthday, she was staying in a palace, and a gorgeous billionaire was in the room next door. Life didn't get much better than this!

Chapter Ten

Thirty minutes later, Brock knocked on Erin's door. "Ready?" he asked when she opened it.

"Have you put sun lotion on?" she said.

"No, but I have a hat." He tugged on a baseball cap.

"That doesn't cover your ears. Wait here." She disappeared and then came back with a bottle of lotion in her hand. Squeezing a little onto her fingers, she smoothed it into his ears, then massaged the rest into his face.

Brock let her, tingling at the touch of her fingers as they trailed across his cheeks and down his neck, and watched with amusement as her cheeks turned a bright shade of pink.

"Don't look at me like that," she scolded. "Sorry. I forgot you weren't Ryan."

He chuckled. "I'm not complaining."

She kept her gaze fixed on his neck, but a smile touched her lips, and he was sure she was taking longer than was necessary to massage the cream in. She stroked across his cheekbone, around to his ear, then down to the neckline of his T-shirt.

"I'll shave before dinner," he said, conscious of the slight rasp of her fingers against his stubble.

She gave a distracted nod, spreading the cream around the back of his neck to cover the strip from his hairline to the edge of his T-shirt that always caught the sun. She'd changed into a pretty blue sundress, and one strap had slid off her shoulder leaving her skin uncovered from the base of her neck to her upper arm. It was hardly an intimate area, but he felt like a Victorian gentleman must have felt on seeing a lady's ankle, turned on because the area wasn't normally visible. That creamy brown expanse of skin bore a white strip like a bra strap, although she obviously wasn't wearing one. Her breasts would be soft and unrestricted in his hands—he could imagine their weight in his palms, and the way her nipples would be relaxed in the warm sun, although they'd tighten if he brushed his thumbs across them.

His body responded, aroused by the thought as well as her tantalizing touch, and before he could stop himself, he moved forward, pinned her up against the doorjamb, and lowered his lips to hers. Erin laughed and returned the kiss, her fingers fanning into his hair, and they exchanged several long kisses before he finally forced himself to move back.

"Sorry," he said. "But that's what you get when you spread sun cream on an unsuspecting male."

She chuckled, clearly enjoying herself, popped the bottle of lotion back inside, and came out with a small handbag. Brock held out his hand, and she lifted the long strap of the bag over her head so it could rest on her hip, and slid her hand into his.

Walking slowly, they headed across the courtyard to the signposted path to the beach. It was a gorgeous day—Brock couldn't have planned better if he'd tried. As they turned the corner and took the path over the grassed area toward the sand, his heart lifted at the sight of the Pacific spread before them like a sparkling blue blanket. The light summer breeze that lifted the strands of Erin's hair around her face teased the ocean into tiny waves that ran up the beach. It took the edge off the heat, but he knew they'd have to be careful not to burn in spite of the lotion she'd applied.

The path led down a series of sand-covered steps, and then they were on the beach. Brock toed off his Converses and Erin slipped off her sandals, and they carried them as they walked along the waterline, the sea warm in the shallows, refreshing to his feet.

Erin held his hand again, and Brock closed his fingers around hers while she started talking about the time she'd been to the Mediterranean, and how it was fairly similar to the Bay of Islands, although with a lot less people.

He was surprised at how much he was enjoying just touching another person again. Sometimes it felt as if Fleur had only died yesterday—at other times he felt as if he'd been alone for millennia. He'd started to wonder if he'd forgotten how to communicate with a partner.

Being on his own had more disadvantages than advantages, but there was no doubt that after time, even though sometimes he hated his lonely, cold apartment, he had grown used to being the only one there. When alone, he only had to concentrate on himself, and he was conscious he'd become selfish. Relationships were often about compromise, he thought, looking down at where the clear water covered his toes. People watched TV programs they wouldn't normally watch because their partner liked them. Wore the clothes their partner liked because they wanted to look nice for them. Ate the food their partner preferred and saw people their partner liked. It's what people did to keep a marriage happy, and while Fleur was alive he'd had no issues with it, but he'd come to like having to please nobody but himself over the past two years.

Part of him had wondered whether, if he started to date again, he'd feel irritable and resentful for having to think about someone else, but for now he felt nothing but pleasure at the notion of spending the day with the woman by his side.

"Penny for them," she said, causing him to look at her in surprise. She wore dark sunglasses that hid her eyes, but she was smiling, suggesting he'd been lost in thought for a while.

"Sorry. I was just thinking how much fun this is."

Her smile spread. "I know what you mean. It's nice to just... be, isn't it?"

He nodded. She was right. Maybe it was because they were older, or perhaps because they'd talked for a long time online before they'd met in the flesh, but he didn't feel any need to impress her or force the conversation.

"You're very easy to be with," she said, confirming his thoughts.

"You don't feel nervous anymore then?" he teased.

She laughed and swirled her feet in the water. "No. I feel better after our talk in the car. I hope I didn't come across as rude because I was hesitant about accepting your gift. I understand your family has always had money?"

"Yes, my parents are wealthy."

"Not having money, it's a bit difficult to understand the motive behind giving it away. My parents manage, but they're hardly well off. When I started work, I was well paid for a while, but then I met Jack and got pregnant, and since then it's been hard. Every penny I have goes towards clothes and toys for Ryan, and saving for birthdays and Christmas. There's rarely any left for treats. I can't imagine having so much money that you don't notice if you give it away. Every cent is precious, and giving it to someone carries meaning. Does that make sense? I'm not explaining myself very well."

"Yes it does. I do understand. You don't want to feel beholden. But that's the thing about a gift—it doesn't require something in return. I mean it, Erin. If we have a lovely dinner tonight, share a bottle of wine and a glass of Lagavulin, maybe have a walk in the moonlight, I'll have considered it money well spent. Although I arranged it because it's your birthday, I also wanted to spend time with you, don't forget. Like I said, I don't have a day off very often. This is a treat for me too! A day without the phone constantly ringing, without having to worry about anyone but myself and a pretty girl. It doesn't come much better than that."

Erin blushed and looked up at him with a shy smile. "You think I'm pretty?"

"I think you're stunning. And as it's your birthday, I'm very happy to tell you at least once an hour."

She stopped walking, and Brock stopped too and turned to her, surprised.

"You're very sweet," she said. Still holding his hand, she moved closer to him.

"Don't think I've ever been called that before."

In typical New Zealand fashion, the beach was empty save for a couple walking right at the other end. Brock felt like a teenager, his stomach fluttering with a mixture of excitement and nerves at this innocent, gentle exploration of each other, and at the promise of a pleasant evening and night to come, whatever it held in store.

"Thank you," Erin said, lifting a hand to cup his cheek. "For being so kind, and for being prepared to take this slowly."

He inhaled at her touch, a shiver descending his spine. "I'm just thrilled you chose to come at all."

"It means a lot to me. Jack hurt me badly, and honestly there was one point where I didn't think I'd ever date anyone again."

He leaned his cheek into her palm, letting a smile curve his lips. "I'm glad you changed your mind."

"*You* changed my mind," she corrected. "You make me feel alive again."

His eyebrows rose, as they were the exact words he could have said to her. But before he could say as much, she lifted up to press her lips against his, and everything fled his mind.

This time, she lifted her arms around his neck and leaned into the kiss. Brock rested his hands on her hips, then slid his arms around her and tightened them, enjoying the feel of her soft body against his. She murmured her approval, a low purr deep in her throat, and the sexy growl fired him up, pushing him to take it to the next level.

Opening his mouth, he touched his tongue tentatively to her bottom lip. Erin inhaled, her lips parting, and he lifted his head. Their eyes met, and for a brief moment he felt as if they were teetering on the edge of something. If she moved back, she'd be saying this was just a friendship for now. If she didn't...

He held his breath, conscious of the crash of the waves, the cry of seagulls overhead, the smell and taste of the ocean. Behind Erin, on the edge of his vision, the blue sky was framed by a magnificent array of pohutukawa trees, their bright red flowers bringing a Christmassy, magical feel to the moment.

Her breasts were soft where they pressed against his chest, her body warm through her thin dress. Brock felt as if it was already Christmas Eve, the air sparkling with anticipation and hope. *Stay*, he thought, hoping his desperation didn't show in his face. *Please don't move away.*

To his relief, her lips curved up. Exultant happiness washed over him, warm and refreshing as the water on his feet, and he lowered his head and kissed her again.

Erin opened her mouth to him, and he touched his tongue to hers, then slid it into her mouth, the sensation so incredibly intimate to his sex-starved body that it flooded him with heat. Crushing her to him, he deepened the kiss and let his passion flow, his internal thermostat continuing to rise when she returned the thrust of his tongue with one of her own and pressed her hips to his.

He moved his hands down her back, enjoying the womanly curve of her waist and the flare of her hips, then tightened his fingers on her bottom and held her to him, pressing his now obvious erection against her mound. Erin gave an unmistakable rock of her hips, pushing against him, and suddenly the sensation of being innocent teenagers on their first date vanished. A very mature, passionate heat burst into flame between them, and it left Brock gasping, his body tight with desire, aching for release.

Lifting his head, he released his grip on her, and she moved back, straightening her dress with self-conscious hands as she glanced over her shoulder to see if anyone had seen them.

"Don't worry. There's nobody else on the beach," he said. The couple at the other end had disappeared, leaving the stretch of pale gold sand empty.

"Is it me or has it just got incredibly hot?" She fanned her face.

He smiled and held out his hand. "Happy birthday."

She slid hers into his and grinned. "Thank you. That gift was even better than the hotel room."

Laughing, they continued along the sand. Brock squeezed her fingers, pleased to see her face alight with a happy glow. That was all he wanted for her—to relieve the pressure of motherhood for a day, to make her feel beautiful for a while.

Yeah, right, the little devil on his shoulder whispered in his ear. Kissing her had nothing to do with the fact that he wanted to see her naked. That he wanted to strip the sundress from her and cover her breasts with his hands. That he wanted to slide inside her, and find his own pleasure in her soft body.

He closed his eyes momentarily against the brilliant sun, unable to argue, and mentally gave the finger to the grinning devil.

Chapter Eleven

They walked to the end of the beach and back, taking their time and talking while they splashed through the shallows. Erin listened while Brock told her about his job at the hospital. She was full of admiration for his dedication and the number of hours he devoted to making children better.

"What job did you do before you became pregnant with Ryan?" he asked.

Erin told him about the publishing company she used to work for, editing and writing features for magazines, and by the time she'd finished they were back at their rooms.

"So I'll call for you just before seven?" Brock said.

"Sure. I can't believe I actually have ninety minutes to myself."

He laughed. "Make the most of it. See you in a while."

He walked to the door of his own room, gave her a wave, and disappeared inside.

Erin let herself in, feeling oddly disquieted. Was it her imagination, or had he been a little... distant since their kiss on the beach? He'd mentioned the difficulty of moving on after the death of his wife. Did he regret getting intimate with Erin now?

She sighed. If he did, there was little she could do about it. She went into the room and wandered across to the deck. A high fence separated her deck from the others so she couldn't see if Brock was out there too.

Leaning against the post, she looked down at the beach, thinking of how she'd felt when he'd kissed her. It made her sad to think he might be feeling regretful. Two years was a long enough time to grieve, wasn't it? It wasn't as if he hadn't even got past the first anniversary of his wife's death. Erin wondered what it must feel like to think you'd found your soulmate and married them, only to lose them at such a young age. It was difficult for her to imagine the depth of grief he must be feeling.

She touched her fingers to her lips, feeling the smile there. His desire for her had been evident, his kiss gentle but passionate. His body wanted her, whatever his heart thought. Caitlin's suggestion of a one-night stand lingered in her mind and wouldn't be banished. Would Brock be interested, or would he decide he wasn't ready to move on?

Erin checked her watch. She liked the idea of trying out the hot tub on the deck, but she decided it would be more fun to use in the dark and instead decided to have a lie down for a while to refresh herself for the evening. The thirty minutes turned into forty-five after the long walk and the fresh sea air, but she still had plenty of time for a shower and to get ready for dinner, and a quick call home to her mother to make sure Ryan was okay.

By the time Brock knocked on the door, she was ready, and she opened it with a smile. The smile turned into an open-mouthed stare at the sight of the gorgeous guy standing on the step. He'd been leaning against the post, looking out across the courtyard, but turned as the door opened and pushed off to stare back at her. So far she'd only seen him in shorts and T-shirt, but tonight he wore smart, dark jeans and a sexy, light-gray shirt that had a contrasting dark-gray strip where the buttons were and along the edge of the collar.

"Wow," she said, unable to hide her admiration.

"I second that." His gaze slid down her, then back up to return to her face with generous warmth.

Erin looked down at herself. Disliking black, and not sure whether to go for smart or casual, she'd followed Caitlin's advice and treated herself to a new summer dress that could fit both categories. A beautiful aqua color she knew complemented her eyes, it reached just above her knees at the front but fell to her ankles at the back in a light gauzy fabric that lifted in the breeze. The bodice wasn't as revealing as she'd intimated, with thin straps and a wide dark belt at the waist, but she knew it drew attention to her curves, and she'd purposely not worn a bra beneath it. Pretty high-heeled sandals completed the look, and she'd washed her hair and left it to bounce around her shoulders, adding a touch of makeup to give herself confidence.

She felt like a million dollars—a perfect complement to a billionaire—and for the first time in three years she felt like a woman first and a mother second rather than the other way around.

"You look fantastic," he said, his eyes filled with admiration.

"Thank you." Picking up the small clutch she'd left by the door, she stepped out and pulled the door shut, then took his outstretched hand.

"You looked beautiful before, but you look amazing tonight," he said, his fingers tightening on hers.

Erin bumped her arm against his as they walked. "I feel amazing. Funny what half an hour on your own without someone constantly wanting you to feed him or play with his dinosaurs will do for a woman."

Brock laughed and pulled her close so he could put his arm around her, and they walked together to the restaurant in the main block.

This was even more impressive than the rooms, if that were possible. Round tables covered in white cloths bore shining silver cutlery and sparkling wine glasses. A waiter showed them to their table, which nestled in a private corner in prime position on the deck overlooking the bay. A deck heater stood nearby in case the sea breeze picked up as the sun sank below the horizon, and a pretty row of tea lights in glass holders were strung on tinsel along the glass barrier.

"This is wonderful," Erin said as she took the seat the waiter held out for her. She reached out to touch the glittering table decoration made from a red candle surrounded by scarlet pohutukawa flowers with deep green leaves and tiny golden baubles. "I feel really Christmassy all of a sudden."

"I know what you mean." Brock sat opposite her. "I'm half-expecting the chef to come out in a sleigh pulled by reindeer halfway through dinner."

"I'm sure he's far too busy sorting out the menu to do that," she said, accepting it from the waiter.

"As long as he's checked it twice," Brock said.

Erin bit her lip until the waiter had withdrawn and then let the giggle loose. "Sorry," she said at Brock's amused look. "I had one of those small bottles of wine from the mini bar and it's gone straight to my head."

"Excellent," he said, looking pleased. "I plan to get you completely drunk tonight." His eyes widened at her laughter.

"Because it's your birthday," he clarified, "not because... Oh I give up."

Chuckling away, thoroughly enjoying herself, she studied the menu, her jaw dropping at the sight of all the wonderful dishes. "I could eat everything on this list."

"You're very welcome to try." Brock appeared impressed by the choice. "This place lives up to its reputation."

"It does," Erin agreed, hoping she looked as if she spent every weekend at a restaurant where the bill would no doubt come to well over a week's rent. "I honestly don't know what to have."

"Well, we're in no hurry, are we? It's only seven. Why don't we start with something like the seafood platter, and we'll just take our time. It's amazing how much you can eat and drink when you spread it over a few hours."

Erin shook her head in bemusement. If someone had told her a few weeks ago she'd be spending her birthday with a billionaire at Paua Cliffs, she'd have laughed them out of the room!

They shared the seafood platter, nibbling at the tempura battered prawns, the maple-pepper salmon bites, and the Bloody Mary oyster shots, and Erin had a glass of Pinot Gris from the local vineyard, while Brock had a glass of Merlot.

While they ate, they talked about everything under the sun, music, movies, sports, art, gradually feeling their way around each other's lives and discovering what they liked and disliked. As they progressed onto their mains—medium-rare Angus fillet for Brock and Tuscan-style grilled tuna steak for Erin—they moved on to talking about deeper things, enjoying their exploration of each other.

Brock asked her lots of questions, and whereas normally Erin would have been hesitant to discuss her personal thoughts on delicate topics, especially on a first date, his genuine interest and the way he listened to her opinion meant she gradually relaxed and opened up.

That might have had a little to do with the wine too, she conceded as the evening progressed. She made sure she sipped water alongside the Pinot Gris, but there was no doubt the alcohol was having an effect. As they moved onto a rather splendid trio of chocolate desserts and then coffee, Erin welcomed the warmth and slight haze that accompanied the wine, enjoying not having to worry that someone might need her.

For the first time in a while, a silence had fallen between them, and Erin's gaze drifted across the bay. They'd been sitting at the table for nearly two-and-a-half hours, and the sun had set, flooding the sea with orange and then purple. Inside the restaurant, a grand piano sat in one corner next to a small dance floor, and about an hour ago a man in a suit had started playing Christmas songs while a beautiful young woman in a silver gown sang along. Now, she was singing *Have Yourself a Merry Little Christmas*, and a shiver descended Erin's spine.

"Would you like to dance?"

She turned startled eyes to her dinner partner. He was watching her, his head tipped to the side, a smile on his lips. She glanced across to the piano. "There's nobody else dancing."

"So?" He got to his feet and held out his hand. From the things he'd told her throughout the evening, Erin had gradually come to understand that beneath his quiet, gentle facade was the steely determination of a man who hadn't got where he was by taking no for an answer, and who didn't care a jot what other people thought of him.

She stared at his hand, her face warming, then slowly got to her feet and took it.

Chapter Twelve

Erin slipped her hand into Brock's, smiling as his fingers closed around hers. He led her into the restaurant, threading through the diners to the wooden floor by the piano, then turned her into his arms and pulled her close.

After several hours of sitting there, watching him across the table and listening to his low, sexy voice, it felt blissful to finally being able to touch him. He held her right hand in his left, and rested his other hand on her hip. Erin placed her left hand on his shoulder, conscious of the smell of his aftershave rising from his warm skin. He'd told her he was going to shave before dinner, and sure enough, his jaw was smooth, free of the bristle that had darkened it earlier.

Conscious of some of the other diners watching them, she kept her gaze lowered, the heat in her face telling her she was blushing.

"Don't be embarrassed," he teased, lowering his head to touch his lips to her cheek. "Every man in this room is wishing he was the one dancing with you."

"And every woman is wishing you were holding her." She looked up, meeting his gaze for a moment, then looked back at his collar again. "I like this shirt."

He gave a short laugh and pulled her a little closer as the song changed to "Chestnuts roasting on an open fire," starting to sing along softly to the song. He had a lovely voice, deep and smooth like Nat King Cole's, and Erin closed her eyes, feeling as if she were made of chocolate that was slowly softening under the heat of his gaze.

Now he was humming, his mouth close to her ear, and she knew if she turned her head his lips would brush her cheek. Her eyelids fluttered open, her gaze captivated by the sparkle of the tinsel around the windows. It was like creeping down the stairs as a child on Christmas Eve and spotting a large parcel in front of the tree with a big red bow. She wanted to sneak up and shake it, slowly pull the bow undone, and see what was inside. Part of her didn't want to spoil it, wanted to prolong the anticipation, just in case the gift wasn't as wonderful as she imagined, but equally she knew she couldn't make it last forever.

Turning her head, she lifted her face a little, and he looked down, his lips almost touching the corner of her mouth. Gosh, he was tall, at least four or five inches taller than her in her heels, and as she moved her hand across his shoulder, her fingers tightened on firm muscle.

They were moving more slowly now, and she felt his hand splay on her lower back, not descending onto her butt, but daring nonetheless, pulling her to him so their bodies were flush from hip to chest. Something was happening between them, she could feel it, changing subtly the way flour and eggs and raisins and cinnamon turned to delicious Christmas pudding in the oven.

She giggled and felt his lips curve against her cheek.

"What are you laughing about?" he murmured.

"I'm comparing you in my head to Christmas pudding."

"I've been called worse in my time."

She laughed, caught up in the spell of the evening, and Brock chuckled, turned her nimbly around on the dance floor, then slowed again.

"You're incredibly sexy," he said, nuzzling her ear.

"Thank you." She moistened her lips with the tip of her tongue, knowing he shouldn't kiss her in the middle of the dance floor, desperately hoping he would. "I'm having such a lovely evening."

"I'm glad."

She wondered if he'd say *And it's not over yet,* or something equally as suggestive to tell her he was interested in taking this further. He didn't, but his breath was warm on her skin.

Erin lifted her face a fraction. He dropped his head a tiny bit more. And then his lips were touching hers, and they exchanged a long, sedate kiss that nevertheless sent her pulse racing.

When he eventually lifted his head, she glanced around the room, wondering if anyone had noticed. Judging by the smiles, several people had, and she returned her gaze to his collar, embarrassed and also gleeful at having been caught smooching in the middle of the dance floor with such a gorgeous guy.

"I like the way you make me feel fifteen again," she said.

"I expect you to pass me notes in Science tomorrow."

She giggled. "Only if you promise to meet me behind the bike sheds."

"It's a deal."

They both laughed. Erin closed her eyes again, drifting off into a dream world. She didn't want tonight to end. If only they could keep dancing here forever, Brock's arms warm around her, his lips grazing hers from time to time.

But of course all good things come to an end, and eventually the song finished. Brock took her hand and led her from the dance floor, smiling as the other diners clapped and one older man whistled.

"You make a lovely couple, dear," the old man's wife said as they passed. "So romantic."

"Thank you," Erin said graciously, deciding it would take too much effort to describe the situation.

Brock gave her an amused gaze before giving the waiter his room number for the bill, and then they left the restaurant and walked slowly across the courtyard back to their rooms.

Although far from cold, the temperature had dropped a little, and the cool evening air cleared the wine-induced haze from Erin's mind. Her heart started to race as they neared her door. What was Brock going to say? Would he ask her back to his room? And what would she reply if he did? She couldn't possibly have a one-night stand with him. Could she? Did it make her a terrible person that she desperately wanted to get him naked? She hadn't had sex for so long that the notion of letting this man strip off her sundress and make love to her in the gorgeous bed made her as nervous as it did excited.

They stopped outside her door, and Brock turned her to face him. He was smiling, and he pulled her close and lifted a hand to tuck a strand of hair behind her ear. "Did you have a nice evening?" he asked.

"I did, thank you, the best in... well... ever, I think."

"I'm glad. Happy birthday, Erin." He bent his head and touched his lips to hers, but it was a demure kiss, just a press of lips, and within seconds he lifted his head again. "I hope you sleep well," he said softly. "I'll call for you in the morning, around eight, and we'll catch some breakfast before we go, eh?"

She nodded, surprised at the intensity of the disappointment that rose within her when she realized he was going to leave. "Sure."

Their eyes met, but she couldn't read his expression. Was he thinking about his wife? She opened her mouth, but no words would come. If she asked him to stay, he might say no, and how would she feel then?

"Goodnight." He gave her a last smile, turned, walked to his door, and let himself in.

The door closed.

"Fuck." Erin looked up at the Southern Cross constellation that glittered in the sky above her, more beautiful than any of the Christmas baubles in the restaurant, and blew out a long breath. She'd practically forced him to state that he didn't expect anything in return for taking her away for the night, plus he was still struggling to get over losing his wife.

It had been a lovely evening, and she had to take it for what it was—a pleasant date with a nice guy, rather than be disappointed because it hadn't turned into a steamy sex session.

She would have loved some steamy sex. But it didn't mean there wouldn't be any in the future. It wouldn't surprise her if he asked to see her again, so maybe in a few weeks' or months' time, when he'd got used to the idea of seeing someone else, they'd get around to it. It would have to be baby steps for both of them, and that was much more sensible than diving into bed on the first date.

Sighing, she went in and closed the door. She crossed the room and opened the sliding doors onto the deck, and turned on the hot tub, heating up the water ready for the dip under the stars she'd promised herself earlier.

Returning inside, she slipped out of her dress and put on her bikini, not quite brave enough to get into the tub naked even though nobody would be able to see her, then went over to the minibar and studied the contents. She didn't want anything to eat and she'd already drunk several glasses of wine, but she fancied taking something into the tub with her.

There were a few little bottles of spirits, and she surveyed them moodily. Brock had promised her a glass of Lagavulin, but they hadn't gotten around to it before they'd left the restaurant.

Perhaps she should ask him if he fancied a nightcap.

Her heart rate picked up at the idea, but she scolded herself for it. How desperate would that look? She couldn't just bang on his door and say *Do you want a whisky to finish off the night?* Could she?

Biting her lip, she grabbed the complementary white bathrobe and slipped it on, shoved her feet into her sandals, and walked to the door.

Then she stopped. This was stupid. She couldn't possibly knock on the guy's door and practically beg him for sex. How cheap was that?

She walked back to the bed and took it off.

Put it back on.

Took it off again.

Growling at herself, she went to the hot tub and tested the water. She retrieved a towel from the bathroom and laid it on the table next to the tub, along with a hair clip, a tumbler and a miniature of Jack Daniel's, and a small pack of mint chocolates from the minibar. She put her phone into the speaker system on the table and chose a playlist of Christmas songs. Then she tidied up her clothes.

Finally, she swore out loud, put on the bathrobe, marched across to the door, and wrenched it open.

She stopped with a gasp. Brock stood outside, still dressed in his jeans and shirt, carrying a bottle of something that look suspiciously like an Islay malt whisky, obviously in the process of pacing up and down.

They stared at each other, their lips gradually curving up.

"How long have you been out here?" she asked.

"About five minutes." He scratched his cheek, then lifted the bottle to show her the Lagavulin label. "I thought you might like a nightcap. Then I told myself I'd promised you I didn't want anything in return for arranging the trip and you might feel obliged to say yes. Then I thought if I didn't ask you, you might think I'm not interested in you, and that is so far from the truth it seemed idiotic not to ask. Then my brain started to hurt."

Erin sighed. "I think we know each other well enough by now to understand what's going on. I'd love a drink, and the hot tub's all ready to go, so for God's sake come in and pour us both a glass before one of us dies from old age."

Laughing, he walked past her into the room. Erin closed the door behind him, filled with relief and a heady sense of excitement. *Thank God.* He felt the same way about her that she felt about him. They were two consenting adults who enjoyed each other's company, and it was the twenty-first century, and it wasn't anyone else's business what went on in this room except hers and Brock's.

Chapter Thirteen

Erin directed Brock to go out onto the deck while she collected another glass from the kitchen, so he wandered across the room and through the open sliding doors, taking the bottle with him.

In spite of the warm weather that day, the breeze from the sea was cool enough to make him shiver, although that could also have been due to the situation, he thought as he closed his eyes and breathed in the warm and fragrant summer air. He'd been on the verge of turning around and going back to his room, certain that if he knocked on Erin's door she'd either give him an outright no, look exasperated as if he'd confirmed her worst fear that he'd had ulterior motives, or sigh and let him in with the air of not having any alternative. Instead, she'd clearly been about to call on him, and her face had lit with pleasure.

His skin tingled at the notion of where the evening was heading. He'd fought with himself for a while, staring at the bottle of whisky he'd bought earlier as the devil on his shoulder argued with the angel on the other side. He'd kissed her already, the devil had argued—that was the difficult bit, the moment where he'd crossed the final boundary from grief into moving on with his life. The symbolism was important, not the actual act, and the next step of taking things further wasn't important at all in the big scheme of things.

But of course it was, and the angel knew that perfectly well. Kissing a woman was one thing—taking off his clothes and making love to her was most definitely another. If he went home now, he could convince himself that he hadn't been unfaithful—that he'd dipped his toe in the water but had managed to fight the urge to dive in, and he knew he'd be able to forgive himself for the brief transgression. If he went further, though, if he went to bed with Erin, he'd be accepting that Fleur had gone and that part of his life was done, and it made him immeasurably sad.

Brock knew he was only human, but all his life he'd fought to be more than the sum of his parts. He didn't want to be one of those guys who used animal passion as an excuse for not being a gentleman. In another lifetime, he would have entered a monastery and taken vows, determined he'd never sully his memory of Fleur by bedding another woman.

But this wasn't medieval England, and when it came down to it, he was young and healthy, and he liked sex. A lot. He missed it—the heat, the excitement, the intense physical release that just wasn't the same when he achieved it on his own, as well as the joy of giving someone else pleasure. But it was more than that, too. Erin wasn't just convenient—the first port in a storm. He met a lot of women in his job, and he could have dated any number of times, but he'd not even come close to being interested until he'd met Erin. He liked her. She made him laugh, and they got on well, which was no small thing.

Plus she was hot. He wanted to kiss her again, and he wanted to make love to her, and he even though his brain wanted him to have idealistic tendencies, he was tired of fighting that basic need.

"Beautiful, isn't it?" Erin joined him on the deck and looked up at the stars. "The Milky Way is so clear here."

"Hardly any light pollution," he agreed, trying to think about something else other than taking off her clothes and crushing his lips to hers.

She put the other glass next to the one she'd already brought out along with a small bowl of ice, then popped a few cubes in each glass. Brock unwrapped the seal from the whisky, took out the cork, and poured the amber liquid over the ice.

Erin sipped it and shuddered. "Wow. I can feel that going all the way down."

He inhaled the peaty, medicinal smell then took a big swallow, feeling a similar burn down to his stomach. "Aah. That's nice."

Leaning over the tub, she tested the water with her hand and giggled. "It's hot. You want to get in?"

He suddenly remembered he was still wearing his jeans and shirt. "Ah, I didn't bring any swim shorts."

"You're wearing boxers or something though, right? Or are you going commando?"

He gave her a wry look. "No, I've got boxers on."

"They'll do. Come on, kit off." Grinning, she tugged the belt of her robe open and let it fall off her shoulders onto the floor.

Brock's eyes widened at the sight of the red bikini barely covering her generous breasts and other more interesting areas. She had a womanly, curvy figure, and it sent bells ringing right through him. "Wow."

Laughing, she sat on the side and swung her legs in, then lowered herself down into the bubbling water. "Ooh, that's nice."

One hand on his hip, he had another mouthful of the whisky and pursed his lips as she winked at him.

"Come on," she said. "Don't be shy."

"Erin, what you've just done, you know how unfair that is, right?"

"What?"

"You've stripped off to almost nothing and now you're expecting me to do the same while you watch."

"So? It is my birthday."

"Do you remember what happened in the car? And you were fully clothed then."

Her lips gradually curved up as she realized what he was getting at. He could almost see her fighting against lowering her gaze to his jeans.

She sipped her whisky. "I'm definitely going to watch you now. In fact, because it's my birthday, I expect you to strip to the music." She leaned back on the tub, one arm stretched out, and raised her eyebrows. Her gaze held more than a little heat.

He sighed. "Yeah. I walked into that one." Putting down his glass, he took out his wallet and phone and put them on the table. Then he began to unbutton his shirt, taking it slow, moving a little to Wham's *Last Christmas* as he did so.

Her eyes widened so fast it was almost comical—clearly she hadn't expected him to agree to her demand. "Nobody is ever going to believe how I spent my twenty-eighth birthday."

"If I see any sign of a phone taking photos, I'm outta here." He held her gaze while he popped another button, more than aware he was turning them both on by undressing.

She laughed, but her expression softened as he continued to undo the buttons. He raised an eyebrow when he reached the bottom of the shirt, and he started to peel it off, then turned his back on her before he let it slowly slip from his shoulders.

She gave a long, contented sigh, and he chuckled and turned to face her, working on his belt.

Her eyes were full of flattering admiration, which only intensified when he finished with the belt. Abandoning any pretense of looking anywhere except at his crotch, she held her breath as he unzipped his trousers.

Brock decided it was pointless to be coy and pretend he wasn't turned on by the notion of slipping into a hot bath with a sexy blonde, and he slid the zip down and pushed the trousers over his hips to the floor. Erin inhaled deeply, and her gaze came up to his, her cheeks flushing a deep pink.

He picked up his clothes and put them over a nearby chair, sat on the side of the hot tub, and lowered himself in. Leaning back with a sigh, he met her gaze and raised an eyebrow.

She started to giggle, and he joined in and laughed, then took another swallow of his whisky.

"This takes some beating," he said. "Sitting in a spa with a gorgeous girl looking out at that view." Night had descended on the Bay of Islands, and the Pacific was a deep shade of blue, the night sky sparkling with silver stars that only added to the Christmassy atmosphere.

"Mmm," she said, looking at him.

"I was talking about the stars."

"Those too." She smiled.

He laughed and swirled his legs in the water. It was a big tub, easily large enough for four people, and Erin sat on the ledge a foot to his left so they were both looking out to sea. Beneath the water, his feet touched hers. He thought about apologizing, then decided that was stupid considering they were both sitting there nearly naked.

Leaning across, she picked up a hair clip from the side, twisted her blonde hair, and pinned it up, letting a few tendrils fall around her face.

He tipped his head, watching her. "I love the way women do that. So sexy. I guess it's because it's not something guys do, in general."

"Yeah, like watching a man put on cufflinks." She chuckled and pushed his foot playfully beneath the water. "I'm glad you were there when I opened the door."

"So am I." He looked into his glass for a moment, swirling the whisky over the ice. "Erin, I meant what I said about not expecting anything in return—"

She reached out and touched two fingers to his lips, halting his words. "I know. Come on, we're both grown-ups. It's stupid to pretend we don't know what's going on. We're attracted to each other, that much is obvious."

He rolled his eyes, assuming she was referring to the erection that had nearly speared its way through his boxers. She laughed and said, "That's not what I meant, but yeah. I know you like me, and I like you. A lot."

To his surprise, she shifted in the tub, moving next to him on the seat so their arms touched. The water came to halfway up her chest, and in spite of the bubbles he could clearly see the curve of her breasts in the red bikini top. He swallowed and tried to focus on her face. It wasn't difficult—her soft mouth promised enough delights to hold his attention.

"The nice thing about being an adult," she said, "is not having to beat around the bush. We're old enough that we can be frank, aren't we? It's been a long time since I dated, but I would make it quite clear if I wasn't interested in you. I wouldn't have come away with you at all if I didn't have a little hope that dinner and a walk on the beach might develop into something more. But obviously you've been grieving for a long time. I know you feel reluctant about moving on, and of course I don't want to force you to do anything you're going to regret later on."

She moistened her lips, her gaze dropping to his mouth. She was thinking about kissing him. He almost groaned out loud. There was no way his erection was going away anytime soon.

She continued, "So if we have a drink and that's… um… all you want to do, that's okay, I mean, I understand if you'd rather…" Her voice trailed off as she looked into his eyes.

"Erin," he said slowly, as if he was talking to a child, "I'm sitting in a hot tub with a hard-on I could use as a battering ram to break down a medieval castle if I wanted. You really think I'm not interested?"

She tried not to laugh. "Well you are a guy, and I know sometimes your brain—or rather your body—and your heart want different things."

"My heart knows perfectly well what it wants," he said, only realizing when he said it that it was the truth. "It wants you, honey, there are no two ways about it. You're right in that I haven't been with anyone since Fleur died, and it feels odd to be moving on again, but there's no question in my mind that I'm ready. I want you. I want to kiss you, I want to strip that gorgeous scrap of material off you, and I want to make love to you. And if that's not what you want, you ought to make it clear right now. Because in five seconds I'm going to kiss you, and once I start, I'm pretty sure we're not going to be able to stop."

Chapter Fourteen

Erin inhaled sharply. Brock's words had taken her by surprise. She'd been so certain he was fighting with himself as to whether this was right for him that his complete and utter certainty shocked her to the core. He spoke with lazy sincerity, and now, as he swallowed the last mouthful of whisky, replaced his glass on the side of the tub, and turned his hot gaze back to her, she had no doubt he meant every word. He wanted her, and providing she gave the go-ahead, the direction they were heading was as clear as the night sky above their heads.

She finished off the last mouthful of the liquid in her own glass, feeling the need for some Dutch courage, and placed her tumbler next to his. Her hand shook a little, although she wasn't sure if he'd seen it. He'd stretched out his arm along the edge of the tub so it was almost around her, but not yet touching, as if in spite of his confident statement he was still uncertain what her reaction would be.

Did he really have no idea how hot she was for him at that moment? His sexy strip, the obvious—and generous—erection he hadn't bothered to hide, the heat in his eyes, his provocative words… They'd all combined to cut through any willpower that might have remained like a laser through butter.

Excited, aroused, and extremely flattered all at the same time, she threw caution to the summer breeze and pushed herself up. After moving in the water to sit astride him, she knelt on the ledge on either side of his hips.

He wrapped his arms around her, holding her until she'd settled herself comfortably and linked her hands behind his neck. The water kept her afloat enough that she didn't have to worry about squishing him, although at that moment she had the feeling he wouldn't have minded being squished.

"Hello," she said, loving the way the water turned his tanned skin shiny like polished mahogany. Her fingers itched to touch him, so she did, running them up the muscles of his upper arms, across his broad shoulders, and down over the defined muscles of his chest. Nice.

"Hello." He met her gaze and smiled. She smiled back, knowing that now they'd made the decision to take this final step, there was no rush, and once again she was back to admiring the wrapped gift in front of the Christmas tree, and prolonging the excitement by trying to guess what was inside.

He rested his hands on her waist, then slid them around to her back, trailing lightly over her skin the same way she'd just done to him. She shivered, and he smirked, clearly aware of how he was affecting her, and enjoying this forgotten power, this ability to tantalize and tease with the promise of sensual delights to come.

Two could play at that sexy game. Sliding her fingers into his short hair, she tipped her head to the left and bent to touch her lips to his. As he moved the last fraction of an inch to meet her, she moved back, denying him the kiss, tipped her head to the right instead, and chuckled at the curve of his lips before she finally gave in and closed the distance between them.

It was blissful to finally kiss him properly, without worrying who was watching, and what he might think, and whether she was doing the right thing. Instead, she concentrated on the firm warmth of his lips, the slick slide of his tongue against hers, the heady taste of the whisky, the silkiness of his short hair in her fingers, and the swirl of the water around her, teasingly warm on her skin.

Brock's hands slid down her back, into the dip of her waist, over her hips, down her thighs, exploring her curves and just, she suspected, enjoying touching her, being close to her, the same way she felt sheer delight at being in contact with a man after so long. While he continued to kiss her, his hands reached her knees, then slowly returned, sliding up her thighs to her hips, spanning her waist, and eventually reaching her breasts, which he finally cupped in his palms.

Erin sighed as he ran his thumbs over her nipples, and when he lifted his head, he didn't have to ask—she nodded, and he moved his hands up to the ties behind her neck and pulled them undone.

The ties drifted down into the water, although the material clung to her breasts as if reluctant to let go. He took the ties in his fingers and pulled them down, peeling the triangles off. He watched as they revealed her nipples, the dusky pink circles turning to tight buds from the sensation of both the water and his light touch.

"You're beautiful," he said, his voice husky with passion.

Erin pulled the ties of the bikini behind her back and dropped the top onto the deck beside the tub. She moved a little closer to him on the ledge, feeling his erection pressing against her through the thin fabric of his boxers and her bikini bottoms. He was long and hard, more than ready for her, and she ached to have him inside her, but equally she didn't want to rush this. They'd both waited a long time to meet the right person to help them take this step, and the last thing she was sure either of them wanted was for it to all be over in a flash.

So she kissed him again, conscious of passion slowly growing between them, their mouths become more demanding, hungry to claim and possess. He stroked her back and breasts, clearly enjoying the lift of them in the water, the easy way his hands glided over her skin. His fingers settled on her nipples, teasing them, tugging gently, and Erin moaned against his mouth. It was no good. She couldn't wait any longer.

Lifting off him, she slid her bikini bottoms down, stepped out of them, and dropped them over the side of the tub. He removed his boxers and let them fall on top of her wet bikini, and then reached over to pick up his wallet where he'd left it on the table. He took out a condom and tore open the wrapper.

Erin watched, eyes wide, as he stood briefly out of the water to roll the condom on. Damn, that was an impressive erection, thick, hard, and long, exactly what a girl would wish for in her Christmas stocking. Her jaw dropped as he gave himself a couple of strokes, then revealed the tip, placed the condom on the end, and rolled it down carefully. Her mouth watered. She wanted to close the distance between them and slide her lips down that solid length, but before she could move he sank beneath the surface and lay back. His wry smile told her he was aware how much he was turning her on.

Well, this was a first. She hadn't expected them to go all the way in the tub, but the feel of the hot water on her skin was so sexy she was glad he hadn't suggested getting out.

She straddled him again, kneeling on the ledge, buoyed by the water, and looked into his eyes. This was it—the final test. Was he truly ready to move on and put the memory of his wife behind him?

Erin half-expected him to stop her at the last moment and say he couldn't do it.

But he didn't. Instead, he parted her folds with the tip of his erection and then paused, sliding his hands around her body while he kissed her, obviously content to let her proceed at her own pace.

Sinking her hands into his hair, kissing him back, she pushed down, and he slid inside her.

They both gasped, his lips parting under hers. She lifted until he was almost out of her, then lowered herself again, and this time she felt him penetrate all the way up to the top. He wasn't small, and the sensation of being stretched and filled was so amazing she nearly came on the spot.

Even more amazing, though, was the look in his eyes, full of heat that burned through her the same way the whisky had when she'd swallowed it.

"Jesus," he whispered, gripping her hips and pushing deep into her. "That feels incredible."

"I know." She rocked her hips, thrusting slowly, driving him in and out of her, aroused by the sensation of his hands sliding over her skin, as well as the silky water lapping around her.

He kissed down her neck, cupped her breast, and bent to fasten his mouth on her nipple. Erin closed her eyes and tipped back her head as he teased the tip with his tongue, then sucked. Screw the hotel and dinner—sex with Brock King was turning out to be the perfect gift.

He swapped from one nipple to the other with his mouth until she was groaning with pleasure, the delicious tightening deep inside announcing the gradual approach of an orgasm. "Brock," she said between gasps, clenching her fingers in his hair.

Tipping back his head, he let her kiss him, sliding his hands down to rest on her hips so he could guide the pace of her thrusts. He slowed her down, encouraging her to move leisurely, obviously with the intention of drawing out their pleasure.

Erin let him, plunging her tongue into his mouth and enjoying his answering low growl. This was the most erotic thing she'd ever done. She'd never had sex in water before, but it was totally at the top of her list now for places to make love. It sloshed around them, keeping her afloat so with each thrust of his hips it took her a fraction of a second longer than normal to come down again, and the surface of the water teased her nipples, making them hypersensitive even when he wasn't touching them.

He held her tightly, starting to thrust harder, grinding against her clit with each push of his hips. "Oh..." she whispered, closing her eyes and focusing on the exquisite tightening of her internal muscles around him.

"Yes," he urged her, "fuck, yeah, come for me, Erin." His fingers dug into her bottom as he slammed into her, and she cried out, clenching around him in a series of blissful pulses that left her gasping and exhausted, only half conscious of the water slopping over the edge of the tub.

He continued to thrust, and she kissed him hard, delving her tongue into his mouth, wanting to pleasure him the way he'd pleasured her. It didn't take long before he stiffened, his muscles hardening beneath her fingertips, and he gasped, spilling into her with short, sharp jerks of his hips and a fierce frown that made her smile.

Eventually, he relaxed back onto the edge of the tub, looking as bewildered and spent as she felt.

"Jesus." He ran his hand through his hair. "I think I actually blacked out there for a moment."

She laughed and kissed him. "It was pretty intense."

He closed his eyes and kissed her back, then slid a wet hand to cup her head, refusing to let her go until she was sighing and limp with happiness.

"Mmm." She placed her hands on his chest and pushed herself up. "Ready?"

"Hold on." He slid a hand between them and held the condom while she lifted herself off. Then he stood and disposed of it before sinking back into the water with a contented groan.

Erin went to sit beside him, suddenly shy at the thought of what they'd done, and how easily he'd pleasured her. As she moved past him, however, he caught her arm. "Come here, you." He turned her in the water so she was facing away from him, then, catching her around the waist, he pulled her back against his chest and wrapped his arms around her.

Erin snuggled back, enjoying being imprisoned by a pair of muscular arms. He nuzzled her ear, and she tipped her head to the side to give him better access.

"Happy birthday," he murmured, placing kisses on her wet skin.

She sighed. "Mmm. Merry Christmas."

He chuckled. "Have you had a nice day?"

"It was a perfect gift, thank you."

"What was?" he teased, nibbling her earlobe.

She splashed him. "Staying here and having dinner. Although the sex was pretty good too."

"I'm glad you think so. I have to say I thought it was fantastic."

Her lips curved up. "I'm glad."

"Do you want another whisky?"

"Ooh yes. A small one."

Keeping one arm around her so she couldn't move away, he placed ice cubes in the glasses, held the bottle so she could pull out the cork, and splashed a little liquid over the ice. After replacing the bottle, he gave her a glass and held his to it. "Cheers."

"Cheers." She sipped the whisky and lay back against him, looking up at the stars. "This whole evening is almost perfect, don't you think?"

"I don't think there's any 'almost' about it." He kissed her hair.

"I'm glad."

They chatted for a while, finishing off their whisky, enjoying the warm water and the balmy night. But eventually Erin knew it was time for the evening to draw to a close.

She held up her hands, showing him her wrinkled fingers. "I'm turning into a prune."

"Yeah, we'd better get out I suppose." He sounded as reluctant as she felt.

They rose and stepped out of the tub, and dried themselves off with the big, fluffy towels. Erin's cheeks warmed as he finished before her and leaned against one of the pillars, watching her. What would happen now? Would he say what a nice night it had been and go back to his room?

"Thanks for a lovely evening." She finished drying her legs and walked to stand before him, holding the towel to her breasts.

"You're very welcome." He looked amused at the way she was covering herself after what they'd done. Unlike her, he didn't bother to try, and she had to fight not to drop her gaze from his face.

She nibbled her bottom lip, watching him tip the last drops of whisky from his glass into his mouth along with an ice cube. Her body heated at the sight of his naked, muscular form. Jeez, the guy was gorgeous. She was tempted to lean forward and lick the hollow of his throat where he'd missed a bit of moisture, then run her tongue down to his—

She blinked. She had to be careful. After all the fun they'd had, she didn't want to ruin the evening by assuming this was more than it was—a one-night stand.

And yet... She didn't want him to go. They'd had such a lovely time, and she wanted to prolong it a bit longer. Was that so terrible?

"You booked two rooms," she said.

He circled the ice in his mouth, his gaze fixed on hers. "Yep." His eyes were warm, but she couldn't tell what he was thinking.

Her heart raced. "So, I suppose you feel it would be a shame if you didn't get your money's worth."

He crunched the cube, his lips gradually curving up as she continued to squirm.

"What are you smirking at?" she said irritably.

"I'm wondering how long it's going to take you to ask me to stay."

Her face burned. "I don't want to assume."

He took her hand and led her toward the bed, leaving the glass on the kitchen counter as they passed it. "You make me laugh."

"Why is that funny?"

"After what we've just done?" He stopped at the foot of the bed and turned her to face him, took her towel, and tossed it over a nearby chair. Then he pulled her into his arms.

"I know..." Her nipples tingled where his chest hair teased them. "But even so, I thought maybe we'd completed our transaction and you'd want to..." She bit her lip at the look on his face. "Why are you glaring at me?"

"I think you should get into bed before I put you over my knee."

"Even if you—" Her voice trailed off as his words sank in. "I'm sorry, what?" Her face burned. Was he into kinky stuff? Because she totally wasn't. Was she? She'd never tried any flavor other than vanilla. She wouldn't like being tied up and sexually tortured by this man at all. Restrained and forced to lie there while he did all kinds of erotic, unimaginable things to her with his hands and mouth...

Holy moly.

He raised his eyebrows as she continued to stare at him. "Erin, it was a turn of phrase."

"Oh."

"You've gone completely scarlet."

"I was thinking about handcuffs… and… licking… " The words came out before she could stop them. Her face burned even hotter. "Damn it. I wish I could stop speaking."

He closed his eyes for a moment. "For the love of God, get into bed before I do something I regret."

She scuttled under the bedclothes, not quite sure whether he was angry or upset. "Sorry."

Shaking his head, he crossed the room and went out onto the deck, retrieved their phones and his wallet, and came back in. He closed the sliding doors, but left the gauzy curtains open so they could look at the stars.

When he turned and walked back, she realized that he wasn't angry or upset. The impressive erection he was sporting suggested he was something else altogether.

He put their phones and his wallet on the bedside table and climbed onto the bed beside her. Pushing her onto her side away from him, he stuffed the sheet between them and pulled her close.

"Ooh," she said, feeling the broom handle digging into her bottom.

"Go to sleep," he scolded, amused. "You're intoxicated."

I'm not so drunk that I'm not aware I'm already crazy about you.

Luckily, this time the words stayed in her head. Listening to him mumbling something about irrepressible women who deserved everything they had coming to them, she let her lips curve in the semi-darkness, sighed blissfully as he kissed her ear, then closed her eyes.

Chapter Fifteen

When Brock awoke, the sky was growing light in the east, and he knew without having to check his phone that it was around his normal rising time of five thirty. Old habits die hard, he thought, even when he'd drunk more than he should have. His head was muzzy, his mouth dry.

The room was large enough not to be stuffy, but even so he felt hot and sticky beneath the sheet, only realizing as he went to roll over and found he couldn't that it was because he had a soft, curvy woman pinned against him.

Erin.

Everything came rushing back—the lovely evening they'd spent together, the way he'd agonized for ages over whether to knock on her door, the tiny red bikini that had driven him insane, and the long, luxurious sex session they'd had in the tub.

Wow.

He shifted onto his back. Erin stirred but didn't move away, still draped over him, her breasts soft pillows against his ribcage, her thigh silkily smooth against his. He smiled in the semi-darkness. Although Fleur had been affectionate, in bed she hadn't been a snuggler, and more often than not he'd woken to find her on her side facing away from him, so it was nice to be with a woman who felt the same way.

A sudden wave of disloyalty washed over him, unexpected and intense, taking his breath away. He stared up at the canopy above their heads and then gently disengaged himself from Erin's grip. She still didn't wake, so he rose from the bed. After briefly visiting the bathroom, he padded over to the kitchen.

He took a small bottle of water from the fridge, walked to the sliding doors, and opened them to let in the early morning air. Leaning against the doorjamb, he drank half the bottle of water in one go, then lowered it with a sigh and wiped his mouth.

Down on the beach, the first rays of the sun were falling on the red flowers of the pohutukawa trees. Fleur had loved them, and they'd planted a few in their garden, although she'd not lived long enough to see them flower.

His throat tightened. It had been two years, and losing her still hurt. He leaned his head against the wood. Last night he'd finally betrayed her, the execution made easier through loneliness and Lagavulin.

Then he frowned. No, that wasn't fair, and it was doing Erin a disservice. He hadn't slept with her just because he was lonely and drunk. Until last night, although he'd missed Fleur, he hadn't been tempted to move on at all, in spite of Charlie and Matt's attempts to help.

It had been Erin who'd resurrected his dead heart, who'd shone bright enough to dispel the shadows he'd inhabited for so long. He'd wanted to be with her, to watch her laugh, to listen to her infectious giggle. She'd entranced him with her red bikini, the way she'd clipped up her hair, with her sheer wonder at the hotel and the sumptuous dinner, and how she'd kissed him on the dance floor, oblivious to the watching diners who'd smiled to see them so obviously captivated with one another.

Because he *was* captivated with her. He rolled his head on the doorjamb to look over at the bed, his lips curving at the sight of her sprawled on her front, the white sheet draped over her and just covering her bottom. He could see a swell of breast beneath her arm, the dip of her waist. She'd not been with anyone either since her son was born, and yet she'd given herself to him wholeheartedly, warm and affectionate, meeting his flare of passion with a heat that had thawed him right through. It was all about her.

Brock had a Playstation at his apartment—he found it a great way to relax, as it was difficult to think about anything else when he was up to his neck fighting zombies or aliens. He felt as if he'd been replaying the same scenario in a game for two years, but finally he'd beaten the boss and discovered the way out, and he was ready to move on to the next level.

He'd loved his wife—he still did, and there would always be a piece of his heart dedicated to her that nobody else would be able to touch. She'd always be the woman he'd loved for ten years, and he cherished his memories of their time together.

But he was ready to move on. And at last he gave himself permission to do so.

He pushed off the doorjamb and walked toward the bed. Leaving the water bottle on the bedside table, he stood for a moment and looked down at the sleeping woman. Her blonde hair lay spread over the pillow, and the rumpled sheets revealed more than covered her. His gaze slid down her body, noting the dip of the sheet between her thighs, the curve of her bottom. She looked soft and inviting, young and healthy, and he wanted to lose himself in her again.

She turned onto her back and pushed the sheet away down to her waist, obviously hot and sticky the same way he had been. He caught his breath, feeling as if he was peeking at the presents under the tree before Christmas morning. Her full breasts were topped with dusky-pink nipples that were large and relaxed in the heat. He wanted to cover them with his mouth and suck them to peaks, tease them with his teeth until she moaned with pleasure.

His body stirred, reacting to his erotic thoughts, but he waited, enjoying the anticipation, the thrill of just looking, drinking his fill of this beautiful girl's bare skin, her womanly curves. The sun was rising, beginning to flood the room with pink light, and he watched her skin glow and glisten, like a shell that had been washed by the tide then left to dry in the sun.

He already knew he wanted to see her again. There were obstacles to overcome—living a hundred and sixty miles away from each other for a start. But he didn't care. He wanted her, and Brock was a man used to getting what he wanted.

He moved to the bottom of the bed, lifted the sheet covering her feet, and crept under it. Slowly, he began to kiss up her body, starting with her toes, moving up her calves to her knees, and then up her thighs.

She stirred, wriggled, then laughed. "Brock? I hope that's you."

"Nope." He kissed up her stomach. "He sent me as a special birthday gift."

"It's not my birthday anymore," she reminded him, and yawned.

"What time were you born?"

"Uh…" She rubbed her eyes. "Midday-ish, I think."

"Then it's still officially your birthday." He appeared from under the sheet and kissed up between her breasts to her face. Then he lay on top of her. "Good morning, Miss Sunshine."

"Oof. Gosh, you're heavy."

"Don't care." He was filled with a hunger for her, and he kissed her, plunging his tongue into her mouth. She placed her palms on his chest and pushed, so he lifted his head.

"I haven't brushed my teeth," she said, her cheeks turning an attractive shade of pink.

"Like I care about that." He caught her hands, moved them above her head, and pinned them there, liking the feel of her stretched out beneath him. "I'm going to kiss you from head to toe, then make you come with my tongue. Then I'm going to take you and make you come again, oh Erin Bloom with the sunshine hair and the even brighter smile. How's that for a wake-up call?"

Her eyes widened. "Goodness. You've woken in a good mood."

"I wonder why?" Filled with an exultant happiness he couldn't describe, he kissed her again. After a second of muffled protestations, she gave in and went limp with a sigh. He murmured his approval, then began to kiss down her body again.

Her generous breasts were warm, her nipples soft and swollen, and he covered one with his mouth and sucked, swirling his tongue over the velvety soft skin until it puckered. He did it to the other one, then went back and forth between them until she squirmed beneath him.

"Stop wriggling," he scolded, kissing down her stomach.

"I can't help it. You're making me ache."

"Good." He settled between her thighs, pushed up her knees, and sank his tongue into her folds.

"Oh... my God." She lifted her hands in the air as if to stop him, then let them fall above her head. "Oh... that is just... heavenly. I feel like singing."

He tried not to laugh and stroked the outside of her thigh. "Feel free," he said before sliding his tongue into her again.

She didn't, but she gave a happy sigh that turned into a long moan as he continued to lick and suck her, teasing her clit with the tip of his tongue. As she gradually relaxed, her thighs loosened and she stretched out, abandoning any final inhibitions. He slid two fingers inside her, groaning to discover her wet and swollen, and loving that he was the one who was giving her such pleasure.

It wasn't long before she came, clenching around his fingers in a series of intense pulses, her cries turning to sighs as she fell back and went limp once more.

Brock withdrew his fingers and moved up the bed to lean over her.

She opened her eyes and looked up at him. At that moment, he was certain he'd never seen anything as beautiful as the sight of the gorgeous blonde beneath him with her flushed cheeks, ruffled hair, and sleepy eyes.

"Mmm, your turn," she murmured.

"Oh no." He bent and kissed her nose. "Remember what I promised? Now I'm going to take you and make you come again." He leaned across to the bedside table and picked up his wallet.

Her eyelids fluttered open. "Again?"

"Multiple orgasms, Ms. Bloom. Girls are so lucky."

"Ah… Sorry to disappoint you, but I don't think I'm one of those women who can have those."

He laughed. "We'll see." Carefully, he tore off the packaging and took out the condom.

"I'm serious, Brock. But don't let that stop you having fun."

"Oh, you don't have to worry about that." He rolled the condom on and leaned over her again.

Erin looked up into his eyes, and something passed between them, as intense and fast as lightning. The night before, their interactions and lovemaking had been tentative and playful, and he'd concentrated on being gentle and considerate, wanting to make sure she enjoyed herself and that he did everything 'right'.

But for the first time, all that vanished, and all he could think about was the soft, sensual body of the woman beneath him, of wanting to plunge into her, to lose himself in her. He'd thought the passionate part of him had died, and although his body still worked, he'd been certain his heart would never again feel that intense need to possess and explore another person's desire. He'd been wrong, and he couldn't help but feel exultant at that realization.

It made his heart thunder, and she must have seen it because her pupils dilated, her lips parted, and the laughter in her eyes faded and was replaced by sultry desire.

He bent and brushed his lips against hers. "Turn over," he whispered.

She swallowed, blinked a few times, then rolled onto her side beneath him and shifted onto her front.

"Lift up your hips," he instructed, retrieving a pillow. She did so, and he slid it beneath her, admiring the way it propped her bottom up. He lifted her hair away from her neck and pressed his lips behind her ear, then kissed down her neck and back, following the curve of her spine to her bottom. Lacing his tongue across her skin, he nibbled the plump muscle, making her exclaim and try to push him off.

"Wow," he said, "you're such a wriggler. Talk about make it difficult for a man. Lie still."

"Not if you're going to tickle me. And stop bossing me about."

He kissed back up to her neck. "No," he murmured. "Open your legs."

She hesitated, breathing heavily, then did as he said. Smirking, he positioned himself between her thighs and guided his erection beneath her.

Lifting her hips, she closed her eyes as he pressed the tip of his erection into her and then steadied himself either side of her shoulders. He pushed forward a little, just parting her folds, and she caught her bottom lip between her teeth. Tipping his head to the side so he could watch her face, he eased out, then did it again, teasing her entrance and enjoying the way her face creased with pleasure each time he moved.

"Oh," she said on the fifth movement of his hips. "Brock... "

"Mmm." The sensation of the most sensitive part of his body slipping through her swollen, wet flesh was like nothing else on earth.

Bringing up a knee, she widened her thighs, giving him better access, and lowered her head onto the pillow. "Please."

He nuzzled her ear. "Please what?"

"Oh..." She tried to push back against him, but he just waited until she'd stopped and then continued with his slow, shallow thrusts.

He could sink into this woman's soft, hot, wet, velvet body forever. Except of course he couldn't, because he'd be lucky if he lasted another minute of this exquisite torture, and judging by her moans and sighs, she wasn't far off coming again either.

Relenting, he pushed forward, and this time he slid all the way in, right up to the hilt.

Erin's hands tightened into fists on the pillow, and she gasped.

"Fuck," he said, lowering his forehead onto her shoulder. "That feels good." It was a vast understatement. How had he gone without this for two whole years? It wasn't just the physical pleasure, it was about sharing himself, and giving someone else passion. No wonder he'd felt so lonely and lost.

He pulled back and thrust firmly, and Erin tipped back her head and exclaimed. He slid a hand beneath her chin and turned her face around to his so he could kiss her, plunging his tongue into her mouth even as he plunged inside her. She moaned, parting her thighs further, completely his at that point.

At that moment he knew this wasn't going to be enough. He wanted to see her again, to do this to her over and over, to explore her and let her explore him, to just be with her.

It wasn't the right time to discuss it, though, and so he increased his pace, slipping a hand beneath her to cup her breast and tug her nipple. "You're going to come for me now," he murmured, thrusting steadily, knowing the angle was teasing that sensitive spot inside her, bringing her closer to the edge.

She shook her head and lowered her forehead back to the pillow, saying something that came out muffled, possibly in reaction to the sound of his hips meeting hers with every thrust.

Balancing on one hand, he slid the other down and beneath her, finding her clit with unerring fingers. He circled his fingers over the swollen button, and she cried out and pushed back against him.

It was too much, and Brock gave in to his urge to thrust hard, plunging into her slick, hot flesh. She came then, clenching around him, and the pulses of her muscles were so strong that it pushed him over the edge. He swore and closed his eyes, everything tightening inside, so intense and exquisite it almost hurt. For a short while everything was sensation, heat and warmth and pleasure. He clung hold of the moment, loving the notion that Erin was feeling exactly the same, bound to him for a few seconds in the shared bliss of fulfilment.

Chapter Sixteen

Limp, hot, and sticky, devoid of energy, Erin blew out a breath and mumbled into the pillow.

"I can't hear you," Brock said, and kissed her ear.

She turned her face. "I said oh my God, oh my God, oh my God."

He laughed, carefully withdrew, disposed of the condom, and collapsed onto the bed beside her. "Come here."

"I can't move. I'll never be able to move again. You've literally shagged me senseless."

"Erin, come here, you daft girl. I want to give you a hug."

She shifted onto her side with a groan, but moved happily beneath his raised arm and into his embrace. "Wow," she said, "You're something."

"Thank you, sweetheart. You too."

"I mean it. You're really something." She meant every word. Sex in the tub had been sensual and exciting, but tinged with the self-consciousness that always accompanies a first time. Brock had been gentle and considerate, and she certainly hadn't had any complaints, but she'd had the feeling taking the step had been difficult for him, and he'd kept a little piece of himself behind. That was okay—she'd expected it would take a long time for him to move on, thinking that maybe he'd never be able to, and he'd always be comparing his first wife to the other women he went with.

She couldn't have been more wrong. There'd been no hesitation in his eyes, no reluctance or awkwardness as he'd said *I'm going to kiss you from head to toe, then make you come with my tongue. Then I'm going to take you and make you come again.* She quivered just to think about those words and the heat in his eyes. At that moment, she knew he'd given her a hundred percent of himself. Up until then, she'd thought him sexy and gorgeous, but it was only when he'd turned her over and taken her with such insistent passion that she felt she'd seen the real Brock shine through.

He kissed her hair. "I hope it means that when I ask you if I can see you again, you'll say yes."

Erin's heart stopped for a moment. Lifting up onto an elbow, she looked at him with surprise. He raised his eyebrows, but he didn't look as if he'd shocked himself with those words.

"Oh," she said.

They studied each other for a moment.

"You're seriously surprised?" His lips curved up. "What a strange woman you are."

"I… ah… didn't expect… what you…" She gave up.

He took a strand of her hair and curled it around his finger. "You don't have to answer now. But you should know that I will be ringing you every day until you say yes." He smiled. "You look as if I've asked you to fly to the moon with me."

"It's almost as complicated as that."

"It's really not." He spoke with lazy certainty. How could he be so relaxed about this?

She frowned. "We live hundreds of miles apart."

"Good job I have a plane then."

"Oh my God."

He laughed. "It's really not a problem. "

Resting her hand on his ribs, she leaned her chin on it. This had all happened so quickly, she hadn't had time to think about the future or where it might lead. He wanted to see her again. Was it possible there was a future ahead for the two of them? She knew nothing about him really, only that he was a pediatrician, and was pretty good in the sack.

"What's your favorite color?" she asked.

He chuckled. "Blue. You?"

"Orange. I like bright colors. I like being cheerful."

He smiled and continued to twirl her hair.

"What was your wife's name?" Erin whispered.

His smile faded and his hand stopped. "That doesn't seem appropriate," he said, a little flatly.

"Sorry." Embarrassment at her faux pas flooded her. "I know it must have been difficult taking that step last night." She sat up and ran a hand through her hair. What a stupid thing to have said.

Brock looked puzzled. "What?"

"I would never want you to feel you've betrayed her memory by being with me." She felt horrified. They'd been together one night. Of course he wouldn't want to talk to her about the woman he'd loved for years.

He stared at her for a moment, then realization obviously sunk in, and he rolled his eyes. "I meant it seems inappropriate for me to talk about another woman while I'm bed with you, sweetheart." Catching her hand, he lifted it to his lips, his eyes warm. "I swear to you, I wasn't thinking of anyone but you while we were making love."

"Oh."

He sighed. "I admit the idea of moving on hadn't been easy, but once I accepted it was time, there was no doubt in my mind that I wanted you." He trailed a hand down her arm. "What I had with Fleur—that was her name, by the way—was great, and if she was still alive, I would have been faithful to her. But she died, and while it was terribly sad, I've been lonely for a long time. Man isn't meant to live alone, and although part of me would love to be heroic enough to say I'll never love again, I'm afraid I'm not that strong a person." His lips twisted in a wry smile.

Erin wrapped her arms around her knees. Outside, the sun was rising, flooding the room with a rose light. Fantails played in the palm trees, their banter filtering through, and in the distance she could hear a boat heading out into the ocean, its engine chug-chug-chugging in the early morning air. Apart from that it was quiet, almost hushed, as if the world was listening to this conversation, watching the two of them exploring each other emotionally the way they'd just done so physically.

"Tell me about when you met Fleur," she said. "How old were you?"

He turned onto his side, propping his head on a hand, and gave her an indulgent smile as if he understood that she needed to know these details if she was going to see him again. "I was twenty, she was eighteen. We met at medical school. She wanted to be a GP. We married when she was twenty-one. At twenty-five she was diagnosed with breast cancer."

"That's so young."

"Yeah. Her family had a history of it, unfortunately—her mother died from it a few years back, and so did her grandmother. Fleur had a double mastectomy, but a year later they found she'd developed pancreatic cancer. We did everything we could, but she died within six months."

Erin rested her chin on her knees. Outside the window, she heard the distinct chirruping of a rosella, accompanied by the flash of its colorful feathers as it swooped down into the bush. It must have been difficult for him being a doctor, she thought, and not being able to make things right for his wife. "Were you there when it happened?"

"Yes. She died at home, and her sister and father were there too. My parents and brothers were in the room next door."

The rosy rays of the sun had turned his skin a warm amber and the silver streaks in his dark hair to gold. Erin let silence settle between them, feeling no need to fill it. He seemed relieved to be talking about it, maybe secretly glad she wanted to know. Running a finger up her leg, he traced her shin, circled her knee, then returned to her foot, apparently enjoying just touching her, just being alive.

"What do you think Ryan will think about us seeing each other?" he asked. "He doesn't see his father at all?"

She shook her head. "They've never met."

He frowned. "I can't get my head around that. Not wanting kids and then finding out your girlfriend is pregnant is one thing—I can understand initial anger and resentment. But after that... what's the point in carrying on that anger?"

"He still thinks I did it on purpose."

"That in itself makes me want to punch him, but I stand by my statement. Even if that were the case and he decided he didn't want to be with you, that's no excuse for shirking his responsibilities. He's a... um..."

"Fucking idiot?"

He laughed. "I was going to say rogue but it sounded a bit nineteenth century. Your description sounds appropriate."

"No, you're right. He is a rogue. He's No Good, as my mother would say. But I've done my crying over him, and over the situation. He's Ryan's biological father, that's all." She turned and lay back down, resting her head on her hand the same way he was. "I've long come to the conclusion that blood is one of the least important things when it comes to bringing up children. I'm not saying it's better for kids to be in a single parent family, and I do think Ryan would benefit from having a father figure around. Kids learn by mimicking their parents, and although obviously I can teach Ryan how to shave when he grows up, I can't teach him how to be a man. He'll have to learn that for himself, and part of me is ashamed I couldn't work things out with his dad for him."

"Sounds like he's better off without him," Brock said with a snort.

"Yeah. Maybe."

His expression softened. "I'm sorry, that was an insensitive thing to say after you've been so nice listening to me rattle on about my wife. I'm sure you still have feelings for the guy, even if he was a dick."

"I have no positive feelings for Jack whatsoever," Erin said vehemently. "You don't have to worry about that. I'm embarrassed that I ever slept with the man."

"Why did you sleep with him?" Brock asked, amused.

"He's a good looking guy. Or was—I haven't seen him for three years. And he knew how to put on an act, how to pretend to be a good guy. He was attentive and charming, and made me feel like the only woman in the world." To her surprise, her voice caught. Wow. She hadn't realized the rat still had an effect on her.

Looking down at the duvet, she traced a finger around the pattern of a flower. She'd had no clue that Jack wasn't the honest gentleman he'd made himself out to be until she'd gotten herself pregnant. She hated that she'd been so gullible. It had undermined her natural ability to trust everyone she met, and she disliked that it had made her wary of people.

Brock slipped a finger beneath her chin and lifted it until she met his eyes. "I'm not like that," he said softly.

She thought of how he'd travelled all the way to Whangarei to give her son a present, and how he'd given her such a lovely birthday gift. True, she had given herself in exchange, but he hadn't asked her to do that. "I know," she said, trying not to think about her mother's words. *You know he only wants one thing, Erin. And a man with money knows how to get it.*

"I mean it," he protested. "I don't claim to be perfect by any means, but I'd never treat a woman—anyone in fact—like that."

"I know." Her smile was natural, and she leaned forward to kiss him.

Catching hold of her, he lay back on the pillows, pulling her with him, and they indulged in a long kiss.

"Mmm," he murmured, wrapping his arms around her. "I could get used to this."

So could I. Erin thought the words, but didn't say them. She'd been so badly hurt before, and it had made her so wary. Brock wasn't anything like Jack, and yet somehow he was—both men were used to getting their own way, and ultimately however she phrased it, Brock had manipulated her into coming away with him.

It's not the same, she told herself as they looked out at the rising sun. But the uneasy feeling persisted, and wouldn't go away.

Chapter Seventeen

Once again, Erin was quiet in the car while Brock drove.

He puzzled on it as he navigated the winding roads along the peninsula back to Kerikeri. He thought she'd enjoyed herself the night before. And again that morning. He smirked to himself at the memory of their lovemaking, and how he'd made her come not once but twice as the sun came up before they finally decided they should get ready for breakfast.

In spite of that, she hadn't responded to his suggestion of seeing each other again with the enthusiasm he'd hoped for. They'd gone for breakfast and had moved on to talking about other things, and so far he hadn't returned to the subject. Part of him didn't want to, afraid she would turn him down. But he'd always been the sort of guy to tackle things head on, and so as they took the turn from the peninsula onto the main road back to Kerikeri, he broached it again.

"What are you up to next weekend?"

She continued to look out of the window. "Not sure. Christmas shopping, I suppose. Should take all of two minutes," she added in a mumble he thought he probably wasn't supposed to hear.

"So… you'll be free to come out with me again?"

"Um…" She looked down at her hands in her lap.

"The thing is, attached to Auckland Zoo is a company called Sleigh Ride. It takes kids to the 'North Pole'." He put air quotes around it. "They get to meet Santa, and there are lots of Christmassy events going on with penguins and carols and stuff. I thought Ryan might like it."

She lifted her big blue eyes to his. "You want us to come to Auckland?"

"I'll pick you up Saturday morning and we'll fly down. Go to the zoo. You can stay with me Saturday night in my apartment, and fly back Sunday."

"Fly down?" she said faintly. "There wouldn't be flights available this late."

"I have my own plane, Erin. I told you that. How do you think I got up here yesterday?"

"I assumed you drove in this car."

"It's a hire car. Far too dull for me. I prefer my F-type Jag." He took the turning for the town center, opened his mouth to tell her about his other cars, saw the look on her face, and closed it again. "What?"

"I can't get my head around this. F-type Jags, private jets, flying here, there, and everywhere. Staying in expensive hotels, eating steak, drinking champagne. It's not part of my life, Brock—it's all completely alien to me." Her eyes were wide, and she looked slightly panicky.

He moved his gaze back to the road. "I understand it might not be what you're used to. I don't understand why it scares you. It's just money. I happen to have more of it than you. Why is it a problem?"

She picked at a nail. "It was just something my mum said."

"What?"

She shook her head.

Leaving it for a moment, he threaded through the town center, then turned left and headed down the hill to the road where she lived. Nowhere in Kerikeri was really rough, but the houses in this area were mainly rundown rentals, the cars old and battered, motorbikes rusting out the front, the lawns unkempt. A group of teenagers studied them moodily as they passed, beer bottles in a pile by their feet—not a great example for the younger kids playing with skateboards further down the street.

Stopping outside her house, he unclipped his seatbelt, then turned off the engine. "Can I come in?"

She stared at him. "Why?"

"I'd like to meet Ryan."

"You've already met him."

"Yeah, but he doesn't know that."

She blinked. "Brock…"

"Please." He spoke firmly. He wasn't going to let her wriggle out of this. Undoubtedly, her mother was looking after Ryan while Erin was away, and he needed to talk to her.

Sighing, she tucked her hair behind her ear. She wore it down today, and it fell past her shoulders in a blonde curtain. Everything about this woman reminded him of sunshine.

"It's just..." She sighed again. "The house, it's... very small. Untidy. I don't have much, Brock."

She met his eyes and then dropped her gaze. She was ashamed.

It wasn't until that moment that he really understood the vast gulf between them where money was concerned. Nor how closely linked poverty and pride were. He felt horrified and hurt that she didn't want him to see where she lived, maybe because she thought he'd laugh, or look down at her for putting up with so little. But there was no point in expressing that hurt. This wasn't about him, and she'd have no idea how she'd just insulted him.

"Less for me to trip over," he said, keeping his voice light. "Come on, I want to meet that son of yours for real and see what he's made out of that Lego I got him."

She raised her gaze to his again. Her lips curved a little, and then she lifted her chin and took a deep breath. "Okay. Come on."

They got out, and he retrieved her bag from the back and locked the car, hoping the wheels would still be there when he came back.

Taking her hand, he walked with her to the door, and she let herself in. "Hi, it's me," she called.

Brock left her bag in the hall and followed her into the living room. Compared to his apartment, the place was tiny, and the furniture consisted of a chocolate-brown sofa and two navy blue chairs, a pine coffee table that had seen better days, a TV so small he'd have hesitated to use it as a PC monitor, and a variety of other bits and pieces that told him everything had either been donated to her by relatives or bought second-hand.

He ignored all that, however, and smiled at the tall, blonde-haired woman who looked like an older version of Erin as she walked forward from the kitchen.

"Mum, this is Brock," Erin said, her cheeks flushing. "Brock, this is my mum—Karen Bloom."

"Lovely to meet you, Karen." He held out his hand.

The older woman shook it. A smile crossed her face, but her eyes were cautious. "Good to meet you too," she said. "And thank you for giving my daughter such a nice birthday gift."

"Mum," Erin warned, confirming his suspicion that Karen wasn't referring to the hotel.

He met Karen's eyes. After what Erin's ex had put her through, he understood that Karen was protective of her, even though he didn't much care for her tarring him with the same brush.

It sounded as if Jack had been the smooth-talking type who'd used his looks to disarm and win women over. While Brock wasn't averse to using his charm, he sensed that in this situation Karen was far too sharp for that, and what she wanted was reassurance that Brock wouldn't dazzle her daughter with money before dropping her like a greased rugby ball.

"You're welcome," he said easily. "I hadn't been there before, but I was very impressed. The hotel was superb, and our rooms were amazing, weren't they?"

Erin nodded, obviously recognizing his use of the plural. No doubt she'd confess to her mother later they'd stayed in the same room, but at least she knew he wasn't going to brag about it. "It was fantastic," she said to Karen. "My room was bigger than this house. It had gorgeous rimu floors and a view right over the bay."

"Mine had a hot tub on the deck," he said, unable to add innocently, "I think yours did too, didn't it?"

Luckily, Karen had turned away to the door, so she missed Erin's reproachful glare. "Ryan's just woken from his nap," Karen said as the boy cried out. "He must have heard the door. You want me to get him?"

"No, I'll go." Erin moved past them, saying over her shoulder, "I won't be long."

Brock watched her go, hiding a smile. Once she disappeared, he looked back at Karen.

She was watching him, and her smile had faded. Slowly, she ran her gaze down him as if assessing him. He shoved his hands in the pockets of his jeans and let her peruse him, refusing to feel like a fifteen-year-old.

When her gaze returned to his, he was smiling.

"Okay?" he said, raising an eyebrow.

She had the grace to flush. "You might have fooled my daughter, but you can't fool me, Mr. King."

"Brock, please. And how have I fooled her, exactly? She's had a hard time of it lately, and I thought she deserved a treat for her birthday."

"That you paid for."

"If she'd paid for it, it wouldn't have been a gift," he pointed out. In the background, he heard Erin taking Ryan into the bathroom and the two of them discussing Transformers before the door swung shut.

"She's had a tough time," Karen said, "and you'd think she'd be more wary of men, but she isn't. She has a heart of gold, and she always believes the best of people. So I have to be wary for her."

"I understand."

"I won't let her be hurt again." Karen's eyes glistened, and Brock softened inside. It must have been hard for her when Jack left, watching Erin go through childbirth and bringing up her son alone.

"I'm not going to hurt her," he said. "I'm going to ask her to marry me."

Karen stared at him. In the distance, he could hear Erin singing Wheels on the Bus, Ryan's high voice singing along with her. Outside the house, the teenagers had found a football and were yelling at each other as they kicked it down the road. Inside the living room, however, he could have heard a pin drop.

"You've known her twenty-four hours," Karen whispered. "That's a stupid thing to say."

"Actually, I've known her over a year. We began talking online when Ryan went into hospital the first time." He shrugged. "I've just got to convince her it's what she wants too." He gave a rueful smile.

"I don't know what to say." Karen probably wasn't lost for words a lot, but she genuinely looked stunned.

"Don't say anything," he murmured. "If I ask her now, I know she'll say no. She's frightened of the fact that I have money, and I don't want it to be a factor in her answer."

"How can it not be a factor? I read that article in the Herald. You're not just rich, you're a billionaire. I'm not even sure how many zeroes are in that."

"Nine. It used to mean a million million, but it's only a thousand million now." He was being dry, but it was lost on Karen.

Her jaw dropped. "How can she possibly ignore that?"

He tipped his head, puzzled.

Then he realized she was assuming her daughter wouldn't be able to say no to the money.

"I think you're vastly underestimating Erin," he said, his voice hard.

Karen gestured around the room. "Look where she lives. We help where we can, but she has almost nothing. You really think the notion of creating a better life for her child won't be a factor in her decision? How naive are you?"

"I'm not naive. I just don't care."

"You don't care if a woman marries you for your cash?"

"Yes," he said patiently, "but that's not what we're talking about here. I had to practically bully her to come away with me last night. I'm going to have to bully her to see me next weekend too. I'm not stupid—she doesn't want me to think she's seeing me for my money. It's like she's made of glass—she's completely transparent. I can see every thought going through her head. Of course wanting a better life for Ryan is going to be a factor in her decision. And it absolutely should be."

"But you said—"

"When I said I didn't want money to be a factor in her answer, I meant that I want to get to know her better before I ask her so she says yes to me, not to my wallet."

"Then why did you tell me?" Karen looked genuinely baffled.

"Because you're her mum. You've been there for her during all her difficult times. She's devoted to you, and you to her, and there's no question you want the best for her. And I don't want you to think I'm using her. She's beautiful inside and out, and I'm going to marry her whatever you think, but I really, really hope you approve of me." He smiled.

"Have you told her you love her yet?" Now Karen looked curious.

"No. Far too early for that." He grinned.

A reluctant smile touched her lips. "I'm not quite sure what to make of you."

"I'm one of the good guys, Mrs. Bloom. I promise I only want good things for your daughter."

"The horn on the bus goes beep, beep, beep," Erin sang, walking out and carrying Ryan as she pressed his nose. He was holding the large Dixon the Dog that Brock had given him on his birthday.

The boy laughed, then saw Brock and stared.

Erin followed his gaze, her expression turning wary at the sight of the two of them still standing. "What's going on?"

"Nothing." Brock smiled at the boy, who'd gone suddenly shy and cuddled up to his mum. "Hey, Ryan. My name's Brock." He held out a hand. The boy studied him, sucking on Dixon's paw, then slowly extended his hand. Brock shook it. "Your mum was telling me how you got some really cool Lego for your birthday."

"It has dino-saws," Ryan said, leaving a gap between the second and third syllables. He scratched his nose.

"You like dinosaurs?"

"Yes. A big wok came out of the sky and they all died."

"He means 'rock'," Erin pointed out. "He's not saying a Chinese cooking pan caused their extinction."

Brock tried not to laugh. "Don't tell me it has a Triceratops."

Ryan gave a small smile. "And a T-wex."

"*And* a T-rex? What about a Stegosaurus?"

"And a Diplodocus." Ryan said the word perfectly. "It's bigger than my arm."

"It's not," Brock fake-scoffed.

"It is! Come and look." Ryan struggled to be put down, so Erin lowered him to the floor. Taking Brock's hand, he led him over to the box in front of the TV.

Brock sat on the carpet and crossed his legs, hiding a smile when Ryan sat beside him and did the same before delving into the box. Brock risked a quick glance up at Erin. She was staring at him, her fingers pressed to her lips, although she turned away when she saw him look up. When Erin walked into the kitchen, Karen glanced over at Brock. Her lips curved up.

Taking that as a small victory, he turned his attention back to the boy, and concentrated on the important matter of making sure the dinosaurs had the right feet.

Chapter Eighteen

Ryan had never been on a plane before.

Erin showed him how to clip in his seat belt, and explained why he had to stay in his seat until Brock told him he could get down.

"We have to keep safe," Brock said. "If you stay in your seat, I'll take you to meet the pilot and show you all the dials in the cabin."

Ryan's eyes widened so far his eyeballs nearly fell out. Erin gave Brock a wry smile. "You'll be his best friend for life the way you're going."

"That's the plan." Brock smiled.

Erin chewed her bottom lip and looked out of the plane as it taxied along the runway. Was he insinuating he was expecting this… whatever it was—a fling? an affair? a relationship?—to be long term? It sounded like it. She didn't know whether that delighted or terrified her.

She'd barely slept over the past week. She'd felt as if a high-profile court case was going on in her head, with the defense and prosecution taking turns to fire questions at her as she struggled to come to a decision about the weekend, and she was exhausted with all the worry.

"I'm glad you said yes," Brock said as if reading her mind.

To look at him, nobody would have guessed he was a billionaire. He wore an All Blacks short-sleeved rugby shirt, a pair of long, cream chino shorts, and gray Converses. The breeze blowing across the airport had ruffled his hair, and she was pretty sure he hadn't shaved. He looked rough and ready, gorgeous enough to eat with a spoon, especially because every time he studied her now he had a gleam in his eye that suggested he was thinking about her with no clothes on.

It wasn't difficult to remind herself he had money, though. They'd walked past the queues of people waiting to board the Air New Zealand flight from Kerikeri to Auckland, and she was now sitting in a cream leather chair on a sumptuous private jet. Ryan sat next to her, Brock opposite, with a table in between. Everything was made from cream leather, polished rimu wood, and glass so clean she could see her face in it. She was terrified about letting Ryan touch anything with his permanently sticky fingers.

"It took me all week to decide," she said, opting for honesty.

"I know." He smiled again.

Not for the first time, she wondered what the conversation he'd had with her mother had involved. It had been clear when she'd returned to the living room after collecting Ryan that the two of them had been talking, but when she'd asked Karen, all she would say was, "It's possible he's one of the good guys."

That didn't help. A one-night stand on her birthday was one thing. She'd had a great time, and she didn't feel beholden to him because he'd gotten sex out of it. She tried not to think about the fact that it could be argued he'd paid a considerable amount for her to go to bed with him. It wasn't like that, and she wasn't going to let her brain think it was.

Meeting him again, flying down to Auckland with him, staying with her son at his apartment—that was a whole other matter. Suddenly it wasn't about a quick fling or satisfying her body's apparently insatiable desire for the guy. She had to think about Ryan, and what it meant for him if she began a relationship with Brock. She had to start thinking about Where It Was Going.

Or did she? After a week of internal wrangling, during which Brock didn't pressure her—if she didn't count the hundred-and-one text messages and phone calls they exchanged in which he repeatedly said he missed her—she became both bored and irritated with herself for not being able to make up her mind. She was tired of worrying about what other people might think if she said yes, including Brock. And eventually she decided she was going to simplify matters and follow her heart.

The plane turned and came to standstill, and the noise of the engines changed as the pilot prepared for take off. Erin covered Ryan's hand with hers. "Ready?"

He nodded, his little face alight with excitement. The plane accelerated, and then she felt the uncomfortable lurch in her stomach as the wheels left the floor and the machine fought against gravity.

Ryan squealed. "We're flying!"

Brock laughed. "You'll see the clouds soon."

"Will we be able to see the silver?" the boy asked.

Brock tipped his head quizzically. "What do you mean?"

"Mummy says evwy cloud has a silver lining."

Brock scratched his chin—she suspected to hide a smile. "That sounds like something your mother would say. We'll have a look out the window when we're a bit higher."

He glanced at Erin, his eyes gleaming with amusement. "Do you always look on the bright side of everything?"

"Don't see much point in the glass half empty notion."

"Some people would say you've had it tough, and it would be understandable if you blamed the world, or Fate, or people, for what's gone wrong."

She shrugged. "Life's hard enough as it is without waking each morning filled with doom and gloom."

His eyes were filled with warmth. He liked her positive approach to life—she could see that. He'd already called her Miss Sunshine, and it made sense that after two years of loneliness and heartbreak, he was enjoying being with someone who focused on the positive in everything.

It wasn't always easy—Erin had her off days the same as anyone else, days when she wanted to curse the universe for everything: for losing her job, for falling pregnant, for not being able to give her child the things she felt he deserved because she didn't have the money, and for being alone for so long. But ultimately, she knew those things weren't anyone else's fault. She could rant and scream Jack's name—and she had done—for abandoning her, or at the world for giving her a tough time, but ultimately shit happens, and she figured it was how she dealt with it that mattered. Negativity breeds negativity, and the last thing she needed was to spiral downward into a pit from which she knew she'd have trouble climbing out of again.

Brock's eyes were growing warmer—he was thinking about her naked again. She gave an involuntary shiver at the thought of going back to his apartment with him. He hadn't specified what the sleeping arrangements would be, but she was certain he wasn't expecting her to sleep with Ryan. Brock had asked her if Ryan slept in a bed now and she'd said yes, but that was as far as they'd discussed it.

He winked at her. She stuck her tongue out at him. He raised his eyebrows and ran his gaze deliberately down her body and back up. By the time it reached her face, she knew her cheeks were scarlet.

Luckily, she was saved by the appearance of the flight attendant. The slim, dark-haired woman who'd told Erin her name was Pat when they boarded came over with two glasses and a beaker for Ryan, and poured fresh orange juice into them.

"What would you like for breakfast, ma'am?" Pat asked.

"Oh, call me Erin, please."

"She won't do that," Brock said. "She's very formal, aren't you, Pat?"

"Yes, Mr. King."

He laughed. "What would you like for breakfast, Ryan? Do you like scrambled eggs? Toast and jam? Cereal?"

"Scwambled eggs!"

"Wow. Me too. It's like we're twins."

Ryan thought that was hysterically funny. Trying not to laugh, Erin attempted to calm him and sent Pam an apologetic look. "Scrambled eggs would be lovely for both of us, thank you."

"Yes, ma'am." Pat smiled and went off to cook the breakfast.

Erin fished out a small Transformer toy for Ryan to play with, and he settled back in his chair to change it from a car into a robot.

"You're very good with him," she told Brock. "Have you been around kids much in your personal life?"

"Only through friends and kids of distant relatives."

"Your brothers don't have any yet?"

He appeared to find that amusing. "No. Charlie wouldn't know which end of a baby was which. And Matt's far too cool to risk getting vomit on his shirt. Mind you, I can't talk. I hold babies like they're rugby balls."

Erin dismissed his words with a wave of her hand. "Aw, with all the work you three have done for children? Visiting sick kids in hospital, making special equipment for them, devoting your whole lives to making them better? And Matt with all his children's books? Now I know you're fibbing."

He shrugged. "I can tell you everything you'd ever want to know about bronchopulmonary dysplasia. Ask me to change a nappy and you'll think my brain's melted."

His smile told her he was teasing her, again. He was being self-deprecating. She liked that about him. Jack had possessed a good sense of humor, but modesty hadn't been one of his characteristics.

"Would you like children?" She couldn't help herself. It was a provocative question, but if he wanted their relationship to last longer than a few weeks, it was something she needed to know.

His gaze slid to Ryan, and she was touched to see his expression soften. He genuinely liked her son. That touched her heart more than a thousand endearments would have done.

Then his eyes came back to her. "When I meet the right woman, of course I would."

For a moment she thought he was referring to someone else. Her confusion must have shown, because amused exasperation crossed his face and he rolled his eyes. "You're determined to make this hard work, aren't you?"

She held her breath. "Make what hard work?"

He tipped his head to the side. "Courting you."

"Courting me?" She couldn't help but scoff. "Where are you from, 1852?"

"Nevertheless. I'd like to point out that it doesn't matter how difficult you intend to make the chase. Once I want something, I never give up until I get it." He raised an eyebrow. She had no doubt he meant every word he said.

"I don't understand," she whispered. "You've..." Her gaze slid to Ryan, but he was absorbed in making the Transformer pick up his fork and transport it across to the salt and pepper pots. "... had me," she finished, mouthing the words.

A frown flickered on his brow. "You think once was enough?"

"Twice."

He smirked. "The point is, do you really think that's what I want from you?" At her wry look, he readjusted the sentence and tried again. "Do you really think that's the only thing I want from you?"

She bit her lip to stop herself from laughing. "Isn't it?"

He smiled, but he held her gaze, and they looked into each other's eyes for a long, long moment. She saw desire there, and affection, and hope too. He wasn't lying. He wanted her, but it wasn't all about getting her into bed. Deep down, she knew that. Over the year they'd been in contact, he'd been polite and courteous, the perfect gentleman, but their relationship—because that's what it was, and she was demeaning it by calling it anything else—had soon exceeded that of a doctor comforting a patient, or of an online friend attempting to reassure a casual contact. They'd liked each other from the beginning, and even though the relationship had developed online first, it didn't mean she could belittle it and pretend it didn't mean anything.

"Ooh!" Ryan broke the spell by sitting upright, having spotted Pat's approach.

Erin averted her gaze and smiled at the flight attendant, exclaiming at the sight of the perfectly cooked scrambled eggs, and concentrated on helping Ryan cut up his toast into squares and watching him to make sure he didn't accidentally send bits of egg shooting off the table onto the pristine carpet.

But inside, she continued to glow with a magic that had nothing to do with it being Christmas.

Chapter Nineteen

Brock had lain awake the night before, worrying about the day ahead. Not because of the organization—his assistant, Lee, had arranged cars and tickets and everything else he needed with his usual efficiency, and the weatherman had promised it would be a beautiful summer's day. But it was the first real stretch of time Brock had spent with Ryan, and he knew this time was crucial. If he connected with the boy, and vice versa, he'd be halfway to winning Erin over, but three-year-olds were notoriously difficult to predict.

He spent all day, every day with children, but that didn't mean he could treat any of them like his own. He'd watched toddlers have tantrums and older children run rings around their parents, but he always stood on the outskirts, left to wonder whether he would have been able to handle a situation any better.

On several occasions, Erin had referred to herself as a bad mother. Brock knew it was half in jest, as the boy was clearly well-loved and cared for, and even though she obviously didn't have any spare cash, the kid obviously didn't go without food or clothing.

However, in spite of her parents being around, Erin had brought the boy up on her own, and Brock could only imagine how difficult that had been. He was already in love with Erin—had been before he met her, he was beginning to realize—but she and her son came as a package, and he was only just starting to understand what that meant. If he wanted Erin, he would need to love the boy too.

Even before his plane touched down in Auckland, he knew his concerns were unfounded. Erin and Ryan had a delightful relationship that constantly brought a smile to Brock's face. He wasn't sure he would have called her strict, but she was firm, especially where manners were concerned, and the boy knew his pleases and thank yous, asked rather than demanded, and seemed to understand if she said no to one of his requests.

Ryan loved the zoo, and they spent a few hours wandering around looking at the lions and tigers, elephants and giraffes, and the petting zoo where Ryan was delighted to be able to hold rabbits, guinea pigs, and puppies.

The boy himself had a lovely nature. Mischievous like many young children, he nevertheless was polite with Brock but also very open, and seemed to take to him immediately. Still, he remained shy, often clamming up when Brock asked him a question, even though he was talkative when his mother was around.

'Talkative' turned into 'about to explode' when they arrived at the sleigh ride at one o'clock for their trip to the North Pole. Rather than being annoying, though, the boy's enthusiasm was infectious. Brock thoroughly enjoyed the whole experience, from sitting in the sleigh while the movie showed Rudolph leading them to the North Pole, to the arrival at Santa's cabin where the icy air conditioning made it feel as if there really was snow outside the windows, to the moment when Ryan finally met Santa.

They stood in line while other kids sat with Santa, even the young ones requesting computers and consoles and mobile phones for Christmas. Brock listened to them, certain the kids' wishes would be granted in spite of the parents rolling their eyes.

When it was Ryan's turn and Santa asked him what he'd like to find in his stocking on Christmas Day, the boy said, "Could I have some more dino-saws please?" at which point Erin burst into tears.

Brock met Santa's eyes and they exchanged a smile.

"We'll see what we can do, young man." Santa patted him on the head. "Here you go." He handed him a wrapped parcel. Brock had already seen some of the other kids unwrap it and hand the truck or the cuddly toy to a parent after a minute's inspection. Ryan, however, hugged his teddy bear as if it were made of gold.

"Come on." Brock put an arm around Erin and led her out to the sleigh where they settled for the ride back to the zoo.

"Sorry," she sniffed, wiping her nose as she watched Ryan introducing his new bear to Dixon.

He kissed her hair. "I don't know who broke my heart more in there. You or Ryan."

She didn't say anything else, just leaned into him as they travelled back to the zoo, and he didn't mention it again. But after that point something seemed to change in Erin, as if the incident had eroded the final brick of the wall she'd tried to keep erected around her heart.

In spite of his cuteness, Ryan was far from angelic. He had enough energy to power a small city and hated sitting still, and he'd developed the toddler habit of questioning everything his mother said, asking "Why?" whenever she tried to give him an explanation. She appeared to have an endless supply of patience with him, and Brock was impressed that when she eventually stated, "That's enough, Ryan," the boy didn't press her.

Ryan did start to grow a little naughty as the day wore on, though, as it grew close to the time when he'd normally take a nap. When Erin nipped to the Ladies', Brock attempted to distract the boy by taking him to look at the nearby enclosure of penguins. The zoo had put on a special Christmas show with them, and although it was busy, Brock managed to find a space for the two of them by the railings.

They'd only been there a few minutes, however, when Ryan looked around and said, "Where's Mummy?"

"She's just gone to the bathroom," Brock said. "She'll only be a minute. Hey, look at that penguin coming down the slide on his tummy!"

But Ryan's clutched Dixon the Dog tightly under his arm, and his bottom lip trembled.

"Hey." Brock dropped to his haunches. "It's okay, I'm here. I'll look after you."

Ryan studied him warily. Then he lifted his arms, requesting a cuddle.

Brock swallowed his surprise, slipped one arm around the boy, and lifted him easily up into his arms. Pushing himself back to his feet, he placed his other hand on Ryan's back and gave it a comforting rub.

Ryan put one arm around Brock's neck and cuddled up to him, sucking on Dixon's paw.

Touched to the core, Brock kissed the boy's head and turned back so the two of them could watch the penguins.

He and Fleur had talked often about having children. Both of them had wanted kids, and Brock would have been happy to have them immediately, but Fleur had planned it all out—she was going to finish her five year medical degree, her two years hospital training, and her three years of specialist training to become a Fellow of the Royal New Zealand College of General Practitioners before they started trying for a baby. That would have made her around twenty-eight—the perfect age, she'd said.

And then, a week before her twenty-fifth birthday, she'd discovered a lump in her breast. Less than two years later, she'd died.

Brock had spent the last two years telling himself he wasn't fated to have children, and he'd done his best to ignore the gaping hole inside him at the thought of not experiencing that part of the cycle of life.

For the first time in a long while, though, he saw a pinprick of light at the end of the tunnel. He knew some men wouldn't be interested in taking on another man's child, but he had no problem with it. It wasn't Ryan's fault that his father was a dick. Brock didn't expect to march in and call himself Ryan's dad—he didn't think either Ryan or Erin would want that, not yet anyway. But he liked the idea of getting to know the boy better.

And maybe, one day, he and Erin would be able to consider having children of their own.

"Sneaky," Erin said, walking up to the barrier beside him. "I'm gone five minutes and you steal my son for a cuddle." She was smiling, though, her eyes warm.

He wondered whether Ryan would reach out now his mother had arrived, but the boy remained cuddled up to him, his eyes drooping. Brock met her gaze. "You don't mind?" he murmured.

"Of course not." She moved closer to him and slipped a hand into the crook of his arm. Together, they watched the penguin show while Ryan dozed, but Brock was aware of her glancing up at him from time to time, a small smile on her lips.

When the show finished, with Ryan still dozing in Brock's arms, they began to walk slowly through the zoo back to the car park. "I'm having such a lovely day," Erin said.

"I'm glad."

"It's been very normal. That's surprised me."

"What do you mean, normal?"

She shook her head as if she'd said too much.

"What?" he prompted, pulling Ryan's hat further down so it shaded his face from the hot sun. Erin had slathered the boy in sun lotion, but even so, the hole in the ozone layer over the Antarctic meant the sun's rays were more powerful in New Zealand than almost anywhere else, so it was important to cover up.

"I don't want to insult you," she said.

"Insult away," he said good-naturedly. "I've had too nice a day to take offence."

"I just thought you'd be flashing your money around a bit more," she admitted. "But apart from the private jet—and I admit that was enough flashing of money to dazzle me for the entire day, if not the whole week—you've been very... normal. I half-expected you to book the zoo so we had it to ourselves or something."

He laughed. "Not much point in that. Half the fun is seeing everyone else's enjoyment."

"I suppose." She scratched her nose. "Could you have booked the zoo if you'd wanted?"

"Probably."

"Wow. Have you ever done anything like that?"

He thought of the night he'd asked Fleur to marry him. He hadn't been quite as rich then—he'd made most of his money since she died and Three Wise Men had taken off, but he hadn't exactly been short of cash. On New Year's Eve, he'd taken her to Fiji's most expensive hotel, hired one of the beaches and the bar on it, and asked her to marry him as the fireworks went off over the hotel. It had been romantic and flash and had taken her breath away, but he didn't want to tell that to Erin.

Instead, he said, "I admit that occasionally I do things to make my life easier, like taking a private jet for example rather than waiting in line for a plane. I rent a nice apartment, which you'll see shortly, and I enjoy wearing expensive suits. But apart from that, money's not really important to me. I give away far more than I spend. I like having money because it gives me freedom, but as Matt's always pointing out to me, money can't buy life, love, or happiness."

"True." She started singing The Beatles' *Money Can't Buy Me Love*. She had such a great voice and seemed completely unaware of how lovely she sounded.

An idea was beginning to bloom in his mind like the scarlet pohutukawa trees bursting into flower around the car park. It needed some thought, and he wasn't ready to share it with Erin yet, but the idea excited him, and he filed it away in his mind to talk to Charlie about later.

They found his car—his Volvo XC90 that was the safest car he could think of for transporting the boy around town. He lowered

Ryan carefully into the new car seat he'd bought, Erin clipped him in, and they got in the front.

"Where is your apartment?" she asked.

He started the engine and pulled away, heading east into the city. "On the waterfront. I used to have a house but I sold that when Fleur died. The apartment is closer to the hospital, and it's nice, but it's not as..." He tipped his head from side to side.

"Homely?"

"Yeah. It's not as homely as the house, maybe because I don't spend a lot of time there, maybe because it's a fully furnished rental. I sold nearly all the furniture we'd had with the house as I found it too difficult to be surrounded by the memories of when and where we bought it all." He sighed. "Charlie and Matt told me to wait for a while but I didn't listen. I thought starting again would make it easier, but it didn't, of course."

"Do you regret getting rid of everything?"

"I did. Not so much now." He was pleased he wasn't taking Erin back to the bed that he and Fleur had slept in. He didn't want Erin to be surrounded by the ghost of another woman.

As usual, it was nose-to-tail as they neared the business district, but it wasn't long before he turned into Queen Street and headed for Princes Wharf.

"I thought I might cook for us tonight rather than eating out," he said as he parked in the large underground car park and got out. "I thought Ryan might prefer that, but it's up to you."

"No, that would be lovely." Erin retrieved a sleepy Ryan out of his seat and hoisted him onto her hip. Brock had asked Lee to take her overnight bag to the apartment after they landed, but he collected the large tote she hauled around that held the usual array of wipes, juice bottles, toys, and snack bars that come with any kid under the age of five.

She glanced around the car park, her gaze coming to rest on the silver F-type Jag two spaces along from the Volvo. "Is that yours? The one you were telling me about?"

"Yeah." He closed the Volvo's doors and locked it.

"How many of these cars are yours?"

"You really don't want to know."

"Brock. Seriously. You don't own this whole car park?"

He laughed, taking her hand and leading her to the elevator. "No. Just this row."

Her eyes widened and her jaw dropped. "But that's, like, ten cars!"

"Er, yeah." He pressed the button to call the elevator. "You know when I said I didn't care about money?"

"Yes…"

"I lied. I like cars."

"So I see." Luckily she looked amused.

They entered the elevator and he entered the code for access to the top floor.

She stared at him. "You have the penthouse?"

"Um, yeah."

Her expression turned wry. "You described your apartment as 'nice'."

"It is nice."

"Why didn't you tell me you had the penthouse?"

He shrugged. The truth was that he'd worried she might refuse to come. He knew his money intimidated her, and he couldn't think of anything more intimidating than what she was about to see when they walked out of the elevator.

It dinged, and the doors slid open. Taking Ryan's hand, she walked into the hallway.

Chapter Twenty

Ahead of Erin on the high wall was a huge painting of an elegant woman in a black evening dress carrying a bouquet of flowers, her hair pinned up in a bun.

She stopped and studied it. "Is that... Fleur?"

Brock chuckled. "No. It came with the apartment."

Even so, it unsettled her, and she'd only just walked in. The woman's appearance summarized everything about Brock having money that made Erin uncomfortable. The evening dress, the fancy hairdo, her pale skin, her slim figure, the high heels, the pearls around her neck... He would be used to being with this sort of woman.

Erin suddenly felt very aware of her tanned skin shiny with sun lotion, her scruffy hair scraped back in a ponytail, her faded T-shirt and well-worn shorts. Of Ryan's sticky fingers that would soon be plastered on every clean surface in this apartment. Of the white carpet he would spill juice on, of the ornaments he would knock off the shelves and the tables he would send flying when he played with his dinosaurs.

"Hey." Brock took her hand. "It's just a place to live. Nothing more."

Erin said nothing and let him lead her along the hallway. He turned left, and they entered the main living area.

A cream leather suite scattered with plum and cream-colored cushions surrounded a glass table in the middle of which sat an elegant vase with a spray of orchids. A tasteful Christmas tree stood in one corner, glittering in the afternoon sun.

Beyond that, all open plan, was a long glass dining table with eight chairs. The pink-and-purple flowers on the table perfectly complemented the purple color of the cushions on the chairs. Behind the dining area, a huge kitchen sparkled with chrome and polished marble work surfaces.

The glass-paneled wall revealed a breathtaking view over the harbor of the City of Sails. Outside, a wide deck housed an outdoor dining suite, a built-in barbecue, and an outdoor sofa and chairs around a long gas fire.

Every painting looked as if it were worth a million dollars. The flowers were all fresh without a sign of a wilted petal. Even the lighting was amazing, and Erin knew the placement of every lamp had been planned to shed the perfect amount of light.

Ryan let go of her other hand and ran forward to throw himself into the cushions on the sofa. Brock laughed, but Erin's heart jumped into her mouth.

"Relax," Brock said, obviously picking up on her tension. "He likes it here anyway."

Saying nothing, she walked over to her son and took off his sandals. "Sit up," she told him, straightening the cushions as he rolled onto his bottom. She took a couple of dinosaurs out of her bag and gave them to him. "Play quietly please."

"Erin, you've got to relax," Brock said, a little desperately.

"I can't." She was almost shaking with tension. "He'll get chocolate or ice-lolly on the cushions, or scrape the buckle of his sandals on the leather."

"I don't care."

"Well I do!"

"Sweetheart." He caught her face in his hands. "It's okay. Marks wipe or wash off. Scratches can be fixed. If something gets broken it can be mended or I'll buy a new one. I really don't care. But I do want you to feel comfortable. If you don't like it here, I'll take you to a hotel."

"It's just... I don't know why I'm here," she blurted out. "You're obviously used to a different sort of woman, and I don't understand why you like me. I don't fit in. I'm embarrassed that you've been to my house—Jesus, what must you have thought when you walked in?" Her cheeks warmed with humiliation beneath his hands.

He frowned and glanced around the room. "I know what this must look like to you, and I understand that you feel intimidated. Like I said, I don't spend a lot of time here, and I know it's not homely. The consultants I work with take turns in holding dinner parties, plus occasionally Charlie, Matt, and I have business meetings here, and it's a pleasant place to entertain. To a certain extent, it's expected of me to have a place like this, you know? But that doesn't mean I don't like taking off my shoes and sitting on the carpet." He smiled. "One day I'd like to have a family home again. Maybe get another dog, have a garden, a pool."

He stroked her cheeks with her thumbs. "I like you because you radiate beauty in both body and spirit. You make me happy. And Ryan makes me happy—he's a lovely boy. For the past two years, my life has been all about work. You two have reminded me there are other things than my job. I can't explain how much I've enjoyed today. So I say it again—if you're going to be uncomfortable here, I'll happily take you to a hotel for the night. Otherwise, please, just enjoy the place. I was looking forward to bringing you here as you seemed to like Paua Cliffs so much."

Erin swallowed hard, took a deep breath, and let it out slowly. She was overreacting, as usual. Brock wasn't trying to intimidate or impress her. He'd obviously expected her to be surprised, but he seemed genuinely upset by her distress.

And why was she distressed? He was right—it was just a place to live, and she deserved to be there as much as anyone else.

"I'm sorry," she whispered.

He brushed a thumb across her lips. "You light up my life," he murmured. Lowering his head, he touched his lips to hers.

It was the briefest of kisses, rose-petal soft, but when he lifted his head she knew she had stars in her eyes.

He smiled. "Come on. I'll show you the rest of the place."

With Ryan following behind, Brock took her across the dining area and kitchen, then through to a smaller study with a desk and leather chair that nevertheless still had a wonderful view across the water. Papers and files littered the table along with a laptop, so it was clear that he spent a lot of his time there.

To Ryan's delight, there was a movie room—a row of comfortable armchairs with cup holders and tables like she'd seen in fancy cinemas facing a huge wall-mounted TV with surround sound.

"We'll watch a movie in here later if you like," Brock promised him.

"Can I have a chair on my own?" the boy asked.

Brock put his hands on his hips. "Of course. You're not a baby, are you?"

"No!" Ryan jumped up and down. Erin tried to hide her smile, and failed.

Brock grinned. "Then you'll have your own chair, and you can put your drink in here, look. And if mum doesn't mind, we'll put some chocolate in bowls and you can put it on your table while we watch."

"Where's my bed?" Ryan asked.

"Come on, I'll show you." Brock took his hand and led him down the corridor, turning right into a bedroom.

Erin's eyes widened as she saw the room. He'd obviously told whoever looked after the apartment that he was having a boy to stay because someone had made the bed up with a Ward Seven duvet cover. There were a couple of Ward Seven toys on the bed too, and a large picture of Dixon the Dog on the wall in glorious color.

"It's peel-off," Brock said with a smile.

But there were no piles of toys to overwhelm and spoil the boy— just one box of Lego in the middle of the bed, a companion box for the dinosaur Lego he'd bought Ryan for his birthday.

Ryan squealed and climbed onto the bed to examine it.

Brock sent Erin a guilty look. "I'm so sorry, I forgot it was there. I meant to ask you if it was okay that I gave it to him. I just don't want him to get bored while he's here."

"It's fine," she said softly, touched he'd considered her feelings.

At that moment, his phone rang in his pocket. "Will you excuse me?" he asked, taking it out.

"Of course," Erin said. His phone had rung several times during the day. Once it had been his brother, Charlie, a couple of times it had been his assistant, Lee, and the hospital had also rung a few times too.

He left the room, and Erin turned to her son, smiling as she sat beside him on the bed and helped him undo the box of Lego. "You'll have to say thank you to Brock," she told him.

"Yes, Mummy." Ryan rifled through the pieces, picking some up to investigate them more closely. "Will you sleep in my bed tonight?"

She cleared her throat. "Um, probably not. You have your own bed at home, don't you? Well this is your bed, and I'll sleep in another bed like I do at home."

"With Bwock?"

Her mouth went dry. She wanted to handle this right, but she didn't know what 'right' was. Should she pretend it was nothing? Keep the boy in the dark and see how things panned out? He wasn't old enough to understand the delicate intricacies of relationships.

But she'd survived this long alone with him because even though he was only three, she shared everything with him. He was all she had, and when she had no money, she told him. When she was worried about something, she told him, because she thought otherwise he wouldn't understand why she was quiet or upset. It might not be the textbook way to bring up a child, but it was her way.

"Yes, I'll sleep in Brock's bed," she said.

He nodded, apparently accepting that. "I like Bwock."

Those three tiny words caused such a sweep of emotion inside her that they took her breath away. "Oh. Do you?"

"He's funny." Ryan clipped two blocks together. "He kissed you."

She held out another block. She hadn't been certain he'd seen the quick peck, but he obviously had. "Yes, he did."

"Why?" He clipped the block on.

"He likes me," she said, feeling a little glow inside at the thought. "Why?"

"I don't know," she said honestly. "He said I make him happy."

Ryan rummaged in the box for the right dinosaur feet. "Does he like me?"

She smiled and ruffled his hair. "Yes. He said you were a lovely boy."

"Will you get mawwied?" he asked, his speech impediment twisting the word.

Her eyes widened. She hadn't even been aware he'd heard of the word, let alone knew what it meant. "Goodness. What made you say that?" She'd told him a while ago that he had a daddy, but that he lived in another country, and had done her best to tell him just the facts and keep her feelings about Jack to herself.

"Will you mawwy Bwock?"

Her heart thumped hard. "I don't know, sweetheart. I've only just met him. People usually get married when they've known each other a long time."

"Why?"

"Because love's like a flower. It takes time to grow."

He thought about it as he searched for the right dinosaur tail. "Do you love Bwock?"

"Um... I've only just met him, honey."

He looked up at her and frowned. "Why is your face all wed?"

A chuckle from the doorway made her glance over. Brock was leaning against the doorpost, his hands in his pockets, watching them. Good lord. Had he heard Ryan ask her if she loved him?

Tongue-tied, she pulled an *eek* face and mouthed, "Sorry." Brock just shook his head and, smiling, walked over to them and sat on the bed beside Ryan.

"Thank you for my Lego, Bwock," Ryan said.

"You're welcome, buddy." Brock found the tail Ryan had been searching for and held it out for him.

"You kissed Mummy," Ryan observed.

"I did. Very nice it was too."

Erin bit her lip. Brock glanced up at her and winked.

"Will you kiss her again?" Ryan wanted to know.

"I hope so," Brock said cheerfully.

"Mummy said she's sleeping in your bed tonight."

Brock nodded at Ryan. "Yeah. That's right."

"Will you have a pillow fight?"

Brock started laughing, and Erin couldn't help but join in.

"I stayed with my fwiend from playgwoup, and we had a pillow fight when we went to bed," Ryan said.

"I think we should," Brock told Erin. "If we do, I'll win."

"Don't bet on it." She joined in with the search for the next Lego piece. "I have a strong right arm."

He chuckled, meeting her gaze. His eyes were warm, and she let herself think about the moment when she'd slip beneath the covers with him tonight, when he'd press his warm, firm body to her, and crush his lips against hers. The heat in his eyes told her he was thinking similar thoughts, and she felt an answering tightening of her nipples at the notion of time alone with him.

"I need his head," Ryan declared, holding up the headless dinosaur.

Brock laughed and helped him search for it.

Erin sighed and put thoughts of the naked billionaire to the back of her mind. When Ryan was in bed, then she could turn her attention to the man at her side.

Was he frustrated at having to share her with her son? She watched him show Ryan how to clip the head on, doing it once, then removing it so the boy could do it himself. He didn't look frustrated.

He looked contented and happy, and for some reason that made Erin happy too.

Chapter Twenty-One

From that moment, it seemed to Brock that Erin relaxed and began to enjoy herself again. He showed her his bedroom, and he could tell by the way her gaze followed him around the room and the sultry look in her eyes that she was thinking about what might happen later that day, when they finally retired to the huge bed with its view over the harbor, and slipped beneath the covers together.

He was looking forward to getting her into bed again too, and it was only late afternoon, but Brock surprised himself by not being impatient for the hours to pass. He carried the Lego box out onto the table on the deck for Ryan, and after pouring himself and Erin a glass of wine, they joined the boy at the table to talk and watch the boats sailing through the harbor as the sun sank lower in the sky.

When Ryan tired of playing with the Lego, Brock turned the TV on in the living room, gave him some paper and a pack of colored pencils he'd bought, and settled him in front of it to watch cartoons.

Sitting Erin at the breakfast bar with her wine, Brock insisted he didn't need help and proceeded to make dinner for them all. Erin assured him that Ryan liked pasta, so he made a basic tomato sauce, tossed it with cooked chopped sausage and some penne, and served it with a simple green salad back out on the deck, because it was a lovely warm evening, and Erin had said she adored the view.

After this, he stacked the dishwasher, and then the three of them went into the movie room and watched a Disney movie on the big screen while they munched on Smarties and Maltesers. Brock sat Ryan between him and Erin, enjoying the boy's delight in the cinema experience, and seeing in Erin's smile her appreciation of his care of her son.

When the movie finished, it was bath time. While Erin ran the bath and filled it with bubbles, Brock showed Ryan the pack of soap crayons he'd bought.

"See all these white tiles?" he told the boy. When Ryan nodded solemnly, expecting to be told he mustn't draw on them, Brock said, "I want to see every one of them covered with pictures, okay?"

Ryan's face lit up, and it was all Erin could do to get him undressed before he got in the bath, eager to get drawing.

By seven o'clock, Ryan was bathed, dried, dressed in pajamas, had been given his inhalers, and was sitting in bed with a sippy cup of warm milk. After making sure he knew where their room was in case he needed her in the night, Erin stretched out next to him with one of Matt's Ward Seven books—which was very well-thumbed, Brock noticed.

Ryan took it out of her hand and gave it to Brock. "Will you wead it?"

"Sure." Giving Erin an amused look, he opened the page. "Here we go. Dixon's X-Ray Disaster."

He proceeded to tell the story about the dog's adventures in the X-Ray department, sending Ryan into squeals of laughter with the voices he gave the characters. As he read, he thought once again how clever his brother was, creating these stories. The writing was simple enough that younger children could understand it easily and older children could read along, but the stories also carried little jokes for the grown-ups reading them, Matt's distinct wry humor shining through.

When he finished, Ryan begged for him to read it again, but Erin shook her head and told him to settle down and she'd sing him a song.

Brock excused himself, saying he'd wait for her in the living room, but he'd only walked a few steps away when Erin's voice rang out, and he stopped, entranced, and leaned against the wall to listen.

She sang a lullaby he hadn't heard since he was a child. The lyrics were a little different to those he remembered, but the tune was the same. "I see the moon, the moon sees me, under the shade of the old oak tree, please let the moon that shines on me, shine on the one I love... Over the ocean, over the sea, that's where my heart is longing to be, please let the moon that shines on me, shine on the one I love."

"Sing the knight one," Ryan prompted when she'd done. So she started singing the hymn that Brock remembered from his youth.

"When a knight won his spurs, in the stories of old, he was gentle and brave, he was gallant and bold."

"Like Bwock," Ryan said.

Erin laughed. "Yes, like Bwock." She continued to sing. "With a shield in his arm and a lance in his hand, for God and for valor he rode through the land."

Brock shivered. Her beautiful voice captured the magic in the words, but that wasn't the only reason a tingle had run down his spine. Oddly, it had been one of Fleur's favorites. For a brief moment he felt light-headed, his throat tightening as an unexpected wave of emotion swept over him.

Then he blinked, took a deep breath, and blew it out. The intensity passed, but instead of leaving him unsettled, he felt a peculiar warmth spread through him. Suddenly, it became crystal clear that time was not linear but circular, and Fleur would always remain a part of his present and future, not just his past.

He walked away, through to the living room, but stood by the windows, watching the last rays of the sun turning the water to gold as Erin's voice continued to ring through the apartment, high and pure as a choirboy's.

Although he'd been brought up a Christian, he wasn't particularly religious and hadn't gone to church in years, but at that moment he had no doubt he was experiencing a spiritual moment. He'd spent many hours in the dark thinking about where Fleur was now, trying to convince himself he'd see her again one day, looking for signs that she was still with him, and struggling to find them. But at that moment, he felt her presence with him, and he knew then that it wasn't about forgetting one woman and moving on to another. His heart was big enough to love them both at the same time, and there was no need to feel guilt that he'd had to leave Fleur behind, because she would always remain with him.

A pair of warm arms slid around his waist, and it was only then he realized that Erin had stopped singing. To his surprise, his cheeks were wet with tears.

"Hey." Her eyes widened when he turned toward her. "What's the matter? Are you okay?"

He passed a hand over his face. "I'm fine. Sorry. You got to me." He laughed and ran a hand through his hair. "You have the voice of an angel."

Erin cupped his face in her hands, her blue eyes studying him with concern. "Are you sure you're okay?"

"Seriously, I'm fine." He closed his eyes for a moment, letting the touch of her hands ground him, the brush of her fingers across his lips reawaken his senses. He could smell her light, flowery perfume, along with the baby shampoo and talc she'd used on Ryan in the bath, and the reassuring smell of warm milk.

She rested her hands on his chest, and he slid his arms around her, pulling her close. It was like having had nothing to eat for two years except dry bread and water, and suddenly he'd been given marshmallows and chocolate brownie and ice cream. She was soft to touch, sweet to smell, a piece of summer in his hands, and he never wanted to let her go.

Lowering his head, he brushed his lips against hers. Her fingers splayed on his chest, then her hands crept up his neck and into his hair as he kissed her, moving his lips across hers slowly, savoring every touch as if taking tiny bites of a favorite meal. He felt her tongue on his lip, tentative and soft, and he opened his mouth and let her slide inside, murmuring his approval. She tasted of Smarties and white wine, and he sighed and tightened his arms around her, deepening the kiss. He adored the way she reacted to him, rising on her tiptoes, pressing her breasts to his chest and her hips to his so she could feel his rising erection.

All too soon, she pulled back, and he gave a long, shivery sigh.

She smiled and took his hand. "We need to give Ryan a little time to get to sleep. Go and sit on the sofa. I'll be with you in a moment."

He watched her walk back to the bedrooms, presumably to check on her son. Picking up their glasses, he refilled them with wine, went over to the suite, and sat on the sofa to wait for her.

She was gone a few minutes, and he rested his head on the back of the sofa and daydreamed for a while, thinking about how it had felt to kiss her, and how much he was looking forward to making love to her. Part of him wanted to take her hard and fast, up against a wall or on the table, to plunge into her soft body until they were covered in sweat and crying out each other's names.

Equally, though, the notion of taking his time also appealed. Of undressing her slowly, removing each piece of clothing one by one and kissing her exposed skin, of trailing his lips down her body and enjoying the touch and taste of her. Yes, he thought, slowly this time, making it last, drawing out the pleasure until neither of them could bear it any longer and pleasure washed over them and carried them away.

A light kiss on his lips brought his eyes open with surprise—he hadn't heard her walk back. Looking at her as she sat beside him on the sofa, he realized why. She was barefoot, and she'd changed out of her T-shirt and shorts into an extremely sexy nightdress. Made of coffee-colored satin, it reached to her shins but was split up the sides to her hips. Quite clearly, she wore nothing beneath it except for a pair of lace-topped flesh-colored thigh-highs.

She retrieved her wine glass and cuddled up to him. "Do you like it?" She'd also removed the band from her hair, which now curled over one shoulder. She didn't wear much makeup, but her lips glistened with lipgloss and she'd obviously topped up her perfume.

"It's gorgeous." He stroked down her curves, his fingers tingling at the sensation of her so soft and slippery in his hands.

"I'm glad. I bought it for you."

He sipped his wine, enjoying the silky cool liquid in his mouth that seemed to complement the touch of the fabric. "It feels expensive."

"It was. Ryan and I will be eating beans on toast for Christmas dinner." She winked at him.

He smiled and slid a finger beneath her chin to lift her gaze to his. "I'd have been just as happy with the shorts and T-shirt."

"Now he tells me." She laughed. "Actually, it was lovely to treat myself to something special. I can't remember the last time I bought a piece of clothing that wasn't practical."

"Well, as I said, I'd have been happy whatever you were wearing, but it is extremely becoming."

Keeping his gaze fixed on hers, he traced his finger up her jawbone to her ear and tucked her hair behind it. He stroked down her neck and arm to where her hand rested on her knee, then up her thigh, into the dip of her waist, and up over her breast, taking care to include her nipple in the journey.

She shivered, and the nipple peaked, showing through the satin like a tiny button.

"Mmm," he murmured, sipping his wine again, enjoying the power he had over her body.

Erin sighed and raised her lips to his, and they exchanged a long, lingering kiss that soon had his body hardening, ready to take her.

When he'd finished his wine, he placed the glass on the coffee table, slid down a little on the sofa so she was almost lying on him, and let both his hands skim over her silky curves while he kissed her.

The setting sun had bathed the room in a warm, pinky light, and the sounds of early evening in the harbor filtered through the open doors—boats heading home, and people calling out to each other as they headed to bars and clubs, joyful it was the weekend and they still had a whole day to relax.

He gave a long sigh. "This is nice." He slid his hands to her bottom and tightened his fingers on the plump muscles, pulling her against him so his erection nestled in her soft mound. "I could lie here forever with you."

"That's a nice thing to say." She brushed her nose against his, then kissed him again. Their tongues entwined, slick and sensual, and her hips gave a slow rock, stroking against him and making them both groan.

She lifted her head again, and he opened his mouth to say something, then hesitated.

"What?" she asked.

He studied her face and raised his hands to slip into her silky hair. "Not now. I'll tell you later, afterward."

"After what?" She gave him a sexy smile.

He touched his lips to hers. "After I've kissed you all over. After I've tasted you. After I've slid inside you and made you come again and again until you beg me to stop."

Her eyelids drifted shut momentarily, her lips parting, and then she lifted up off him and rose to her feet. Holding out a hand, she said, "Come on. Let's see if Ryan's asleep."

Chapter Twenty-Two

Erin led Brock through the quiet living room, past the kitchen, and along to the bedrooms. Her hand tingled where his skin warmed hers, the tingle progressing up her arm and through her body at the notion of his fingers moving to other areas. Lying on the sofa in the last rays of the setting sun had been bliss, and she agreed with him that she could have stayed there forever, drinking in the warmth, kissing and touching him, and being kissed and touched in return.

Still, the idea of getting him naked proved too strong a draw. She paused outside Ryan's room first, smiling at the sight of him spread-eagled and tangled in the duvet, his cheeks bearing a healthy flush.

"He looks well," Brock murmured, sliding his arms around her waist and resting his chin on her shoulder. "How has his chest been?"

"Good."

"It must have been terrifying for you when he had the attack."

"It was." She thought about the afternoon his breathing had suddenly grown worse, the panic that had flooded her when the Ventolin inhaler hadn't worked. Brock would know how she'd felt, of course, because he'd been through it with his sister. "It's funny," she said, "But I thought of you then. I knew if you'd been there, you'd have been able to help him." She swallowed at the sight of Ryan's body, so tiny and fragile. "I feel so useless sometimes. I'm such a terrible mother."

Brock chuckled and kissed her shoulder. "You keep saying that, and you're really not."

She was making a joke out of it, but the truth lay beneath it like bedrock beneath soil, solid and unmovable. Her emotion was real, tears pricking her lids. "I feel it. I know it sounds pathetic, like I'm begging for compliments, but I watch some of the other mothers and I just feel so crap at it. All they talk about is wholegrains and five portions of fruit and veg, and there are all these things you're supposed to do like make your kid listen to classical music and read

War and Peace from the age of three. It's all I can do to get him to sit still so I can stuff a sausage down him."

"Being a single parent must be incredibly hard. I can only imagine."

She sniffed and rubbed her nose. "I shouldn't complain. I have my parents, which is a lot more than other people have."

"I suppose, but that's not the point. There's nothing wrong with being a single parent, but I can see how having a partner has its advantages. You can play good cop, bad cop, for a start. I see that often enough—mum being tough while dad tries the soft approach, and vice versa. But it's also about having someone to confide in and discuss things with. When your parents are there, I'm sure you feel as if you have to put a brave face on and act as if you're coping, even if you're having a tough day. But with a partner you can voice your worries and talk about options. I think you've done amazingly well on your own."

She swallowed, tore her gaze away from her son, and turned to look into Brock's eyes. "You say such nice things."

"You deserve nice things." He kissed her nose.

She looked into his deep brown eyes, overcome by a wave of... what? Affection? Lust?

Even though she sometimes hid things from her parents, she'd always been honest with herself. *Be honest, Erin.*

She loved him.

There was no fighting the fact. She could make excuses—it's too soon, it must be lust, love takes time to grow... But the truth was that she'd fallen in love with him a while ago. It felt odd to admit it, and no doubt others would laugh and say it was impossible, but she'd fallen for his sense of humor, his kind words, his gentle manner, even before they'd spoken on the phone.

She couldn't say it, though. The relationship was too new and fragile for her to open her heart. This was supposed to be about sex, pure and raw. He liked her—she knew that, and there was definitely the possibility of what they had developing into something more permanent. Maybe. But she couldn't bet on it. She had a kid, and she couldn't just presume a young, single guy would take on another man's child. He'd been really good with Ryan, and she couldn't believe it was just to get into her knickers, but that didn't mean he wanted to take on the responsibility of looking after him for life.

God, it was complicated. Her mother's words echoed through her brain. *He'll think you're after his money. It'll eat at him, the same way it will eat at you every time you wonder whether you're only with him because of it.* Erin wanted to shake her head so the words fell out of her ears like marbles out of a tin. But she couldn't, and they remained in there, rolling around and around until they almost drowned out everything else. People were animals, she thought, and their survival instinct is incredibly strong. Looking after and providing for Ryan was the most important thing in her life—it went deeper than thought or desire—it went deep as the bone. How could she be certain that what she felt for Brock had nothing to do with his money?

"What?" He cupped her face, his expression showing concern. His brown eyes had flecks of orange around the edges. She hadn't noticed that before. *See? You hardly know the guy.*

"I…" She bit her lip. She was overthinking this and it was making her head hurt.

I love you, but I don't just love you because you're rich. She wanted to say the words, but it was the last thing she could possibly say.

The only thing she could do was show him how she felt.

Lifting onto her tiptoes, she pressed her lips to his.

She felt them curve beneath hers, surprised at her movement, but he didn't pull away. Instead, he wrapped his arms around her and gave her a big hug as she kissed him, as if he was aware of her inner turmoil and wanted to comfort her.

Still holding her, apparently reluctant to remove his lips from hers, Brock took slow steps backward toward their room. Erin opened her mouth to his searching tongue, hungry for him, wanting to devour and be devoured, wanting to lose herself in the bliss of their lovemaking until she didn't have to think anymore, until desire and passion took over and melted her brain.

Brock seemed happy to help with this. Once they were inside the room, he closed the door behind them, but continued walking her across the room to the glass wall overlooking the harbor. There he broke contact with her briefly to open the large sliding doors and allow the warm evening air into the room. It carried with it the sounds of a Kiwi summer Christmas—refrains of a festive pop song spiraling up from a bar further along the wharf, and distant sounds of conversation and laughter from a firm's Christmas party. Someone had placed a string of fairy lights along the balcony surrounding the room, and they glittered against the backdrop of the mauve evening sky and the darker blue sea.

She had no more time to look at the view, though, because Brock turned her so her back was against the window and pushed her up against it. Erin groaned as he captured her hands in his, linked their fingers, and pinned her hands above her head. He pressed his body against hers, all hard muscle against her soft flesh, and she moaned as he kissed her deeply, the moan turning into a long sigh of pleasure when his tongue stroked into her mouth.

He was already turned on, already hard pressing into her mound, but he kissed her leisurely, as if he wanted to prolong the moment. Erin was half-frustrated, half-relieved. Part of her wanted him to rip off his clothes, then tear off hers, throw her on the bed, and thrust her into oblivion. She knew she'd come in seconds.

Equally, she was desperate to make the most of their time together, and felt a surge of happiness that he appeared to feel the same. He hadn't brought her here for a quick shag just to relieve a physical urge. He'd asked her to stay because he wanted this—a languid worship of her body, and she was more than happy to comply.

"Mmm," she murmured when he finally lifted his head.

He smiled and brushed his nose against hers. "This is nice."

"It's wonderful. It feels magical, as if we've stolen a little bit of Christmas early for ourselves."

She stopped then, embarrassed that she sounded overly romantic, but he just whispered, "I know what you mean," before kissing her again.

The coolness of the glass sank into her skin through the silky nightie, and Erin suddenly realized anyone out in the bay would be able to see Brock pinning her up against the window. Heat flooded her cheeks, but she couldn't protest because his mouth was on hers again, his tongue delving inside, and soon she forgot everything but the way her body was reacting to his, the pure deliciousness of being made love to by such a gorgeous guy.

When he eventually lifted his head, her chest was heaving and her eyelids felt as if they were made of lead. "Now I know what it means to be kissed senseless," she said, panting.

He laughed and lowered their hands, but kept hold of one to draw her with him to the bed. She bent to grasp a handful of the nightie at the knee with the intention of removing it, but he shook his head and instructed, "Leave it on."

Heart thumping, Erin moved onto the huge bed and lay back on the white pillows, watching Brock undress for her. It didn't take long—no slow strip this time. Instead, he grabbed a handful of his T-shirt behind the back of his head and yanked it off, then popped the button of his shorts and thrust those down his legs before kicking them off too.

Clad only in his tight black boxer-briefs, he climbed onto the mattress and crawled on his hands and knees until he leaned over her. Once again, he held her hands and linked their fingers, then pinned them above her head.

Erin looked up at his broad chest with its sprinkling of curly brown hairs, at the muscular arms braced either side of her, and at his handsome face looking down at her with barely-concealed desire, and shivered.

He raised an eyebrow. "You cold?"

"No."

He met her eyes, then slowly slid his gaze all the way down her satin-clad body. By the time it returned to hers, it held so much heat that she was sure every inch of her skin held a healthy blush.

"I want you," he said.

"Take me, then," she said, breathless with desire.

"Oh, I will." His lazy certainty made her heart miss a beat. "All in good time."

She flexed her fingers in his, feeling naked beneath his hot stare, even though she still wore her nightie. Nudging the hem of the silky item up with one knee to her thighs, he moved to kneel between her legs and lowered his hips to hers. He gave a slow thrust, stroking the length of his erection against her clit, separated only by the silk of her nightdress and his cotton briefs.

"Oh." She drew up her knees on either side, trying to push against him, but he lifted his hips, denying her the precious contact her body yearned for.

"Brock..." She shifted beneath him, tortured by the brush of the material across her nipples.

"Slowly," he instructed. Dipping his head, he began to place kisses up her jaw to her ear. "A well-prepared meal should be savored with tiny bites, letting the flavors form on the taste buds." He touched the tip of his tongue to the sensitive spot below her earlobe as if illustrating the fact.

"Ooh," she said, trembling.

"We're going to take our time and make this last." His deep voice in her ear brought goose bumps rising across her skin. Her neck burned from his hot breath as he trailed his lips down it. "I want to take you to that place at the edge of desire. You know the one I mean?"

"No," she said faintly, her nipples tightening so much they almost hurt. In the background, she could hear the song had changed to Bing Crosby's *White Christmas*. She'd not considered it a sexy song before, but suddenly it felt full of sensuality, as if she were being coated with honey or melted chocolate.

Brock kissed where her neck met her shoulder, then tilted his head to kiss under her chin and touched his tongue to the dip at the base of her throat. "There's a moment where your muscles start to tighten, where you can feel your orgasm in the distance like thunder, and it's nearly there, just seconds away. It's almost better than when you actually come, because it's like Christmas Eve, full of the promise of pleasure. That's where I want to take you, and I want to keep you there as long as I can, until you're aching and crying out my name, until you're begging me to let you come because you can't bear it any longer."

"I'm there already," Erin said with a groan, a dull ache throbbing between her thighs.

He chuckled and kissed up the sensitive skin under her arms, taking tiny nibbles with his teeth before following the movement with his tongue. "You're nowhere near it. Trust me."

"I do," she whispered, meaning it.

He lifted his head and looked into her eyes for a long moment. Then he gave a satisfied nod, and lowered his lips.

Chapter Twenty-Three

Stopping himself from tearing off Erin's silky nightie and plunging into her welcoming body was incredibly difficult. She smelled divine, of jasmine mixed with the musky smell of arousal, and for some reason she tasted of chocolate, although he couldn't think why. Everything about her was soft, from her feet and legs to the swells and curves beneath the nightdress to the hair that tumbled like a sheet of gold silk across the pillow. He knew that when he eventually slid inside her, she'd be warm, moist, and slippery, and he was desperate to plunge deep into her and take his own pleasure.

But he didn't. He finally released her hands, liking the way she sank them into his hair, her fingers tightening in the strands as he kissed down her neck to her breasts. Cupping the soft mounds, he reveled in their weight and firmness, adoring how the fabric enabled his hands to slide over them.

Erin lifted her arms over her head and stretched out beneath him, arching her back and pushing her breasts toward him. He took the hint and nuzzled her nipple with his nose, then teased the soft peak with his lips through the fabric. It hardened to a tight nub, and she sighed, a long, low, lazy *mmm* of approval that made him smile.

He toyed with her other nipple until it was also tight, then kissed down her belly, sliding the nightie up her legs as he did so. The tender skin on the inside of her thighs was almost as silky beneath his fingers as the satin material. He continued to kiss over her hips until he met the crease of her thigh, where he paused to breathe in her scent.

"Brock," she mumbled, obviously embarrassed as he inhaled, but he ignored her and kissed her other thigh, only then letting himself lower his mouth to her folds.

Even there, she tasted of chocolate, although maybe it was just his senses getting muddled, the velvety feel and warm taste of her mingling with the luxurious smoothness of Crosby's voice until he felt as if she were a Christmas parcel waiting to be unwrapped.

Pushing her thighs wide, he parted her folds and delved his tongue inside her to lap at her arousal, growing even harder at the rich, warm moisture he'd coaxed from her with his kisses. She moaned and sank a hand into his hair, and he slid his tongue up through her folds, pressing gently at the top with two fingers to expose her clit.

Gently, he blew warm air across it, and Erin gave an *aaahhh* of ecstasy. He touched the very tip of his tongue to the swollen button, and she cried out and clenched her fingers in his hair. His own fingers tightened into fists as he fought with himself not to bury his mouth in her and suck until she came. *Slowly, Brock. Slowly.*

He gave her clit a few delicate swirls of his tongue, then moved back and up the bed. Quickly shucking his briefs, he lay beside her. She groaned but turned to face him, her cheeks flushed a becoming pink, her lips parted.

"I ache," she whispered, lowering a hand between her legs.

"Nah-ah." He caught it and lifted it to stop her, then shifted closer so they were lying face-to-face. He slipped one arm behind her so he could pull her into his arms.

"Tease," she said, a little sulkily.

"Yep. The thought of you aching for me turns me on." He kissed her and slid his other hand down her back to her knee, which he then lifted over his thigh so she was wrapped around him. His erection pressed against her belly, eager for action.

"Does that make you a sadist?" She lifted her nightie and shifted so the tip of him slid beneath her.

He rocked his hips, sliding through her slippery folds. "I'm not into pain, but I'm open to a bit of sexy torture."

She closed her eyes. "Oh God."

He chuckled and nuzzled her neck. "Does that turn you on, Ms. Bloom?" He continued to slide his erection beneath her, arousing himself as well as her. "How about next time I bring some scarves, tie you down, and do unspeakable things to you?" His erection swelled at the thought.

With a groan, she tipped her head to the side to give him better access to her ear. "Like what?"

He kissed around the shell of her ear, then nibbled the lobe. "Depends how far you'll let me go." Lightly, he brushed his lips along her jaw to her mouth.

Her lips parted, her breath warming his lips. "What if I said as far as your imagination will take you?"

He lifted his head and met her gaze, and they exchanged a long look. Brock's heart raced. He'd never felt such a strong urge to possess a woman, to take her and make her cry out his name with pleasure. "You should be careful what you say," he warned, tightening his hand on her bottom as he pulled her to him. "I have a very good imagination."

Her lips curved up and she kissed him. "As long as it's just the two of us, you can do whatever you want to me."

He closed his eyes, counted to ten, then opened them and blew out a breath. "Fucking hell, Erin. I'm trying to make this last."

"You started it." Hooking her leg over his hip, she moved until the tip of his erection sank inside her.

Still trying to keep control, he gave her a warning look. "Condom," he said, about to roll onto his back to retrieve one from the bedside table.

She caught his arm and stopped him moving. "I'm on the pill." She kissed him. "If you don't want to use a condom, I don't mind. It's up to you."

The notion of sliding inside her without barriers was too tempting to ignore. She'd completely turned the tables on him, and now it was him fighting for control, his body aching for release. "You're sure?" His voice sounded hoarse, even to him. When she nodded, he pushed his hips forward and slowly sheathed himself in her.

"*Aaahhh...*" He rested his forehead against hers and closed his eyes again. Man, that felt good.

She rocked her hips to make sure he was coated with her moisture, then shifted on the bed so she was pressed against him from belly to chest, letting him slide deep inside.

He opened his eyes and kissed her, reveling in the sensation of her soft body wrapped around him, her skin warm beneath the satin. Their tongues swirled and tangled while their hips moved in unison, teasing sensation from them and gradually encouraging them closer to the edge.

"Easy," he said, sliding his hand to her bottom to slow down her hips.

"I can't... it's too... *ooohhh...*"

He teased her lips with his and nibbled them with his teeth, then ran his tongue along them. "Too…"

"Mmm," she murmured, apparently unable to articulate how she was feeling. Her nails dug into his shoulder, and she scraped them lightly down his back, making him shiver. Her eyelids drifted shut, but he nudged her cheek with his nose.

"Open," he instructed.

They fluttered open, her blue eyes sleepy with desire. "Why?"

"I want you to look at me when you come."

"Why?" she whispered, unwittingly echoing her son's tendency to question.

"So I'm sure you're thinking of me." He was close to coming himself, muscles tightening deep inside, his balls aching for release, but he tried to hold it in, wanting her to come with him.

"There's only you." Her blue eyes were clear and honest, her lips parting as her breath came in ragged pants. "I think there's only ever been you, Brock."

He was barely moving now, conscious that every cell in his body seemed hyper-sensitive. He consisted only of nerve endings, reacting to every touch of her hands, kiss of her lips, and miniscule thrust of her hips that sent him sliding in and out of her, arousing him with every stroke.

Brushing up her body to her breast, he teased her nipple, and her eyelids fluttered shut again before re-opening as she obviously remembered his instructions.

He looked into the eyes of this girl he'd fallen for even before he'd met her, and although he'd been going to wait until after they'd finished, as everything began to tighten, he couldn't stop the words falling out. "I love you."

There was no time to wait for her reaction. Heat spread up through him, and he crushed his lips to hers and pulled her tight against him as he spilled into her with intense pulses. Erin moaned against his lips and then he felt her contract around him, her internal muscles milking every last drop out of him as she came. They clenched together in a paroxysm of bliss, and he looked deep into her eyes, convincing himself that she would never, as long as he lived, belong to anyone else.

The pulses slowed, their muscles relaxed, and Brock gave a long, happy sigh. Rolling onto his back, still inside her, he brought her with him so she lay on top of him, and slid a hand into her hair to bring her head down so he could capture her lips for a long kiss.

When he eventually released her, she propped herself up on her elbows and studied him. "Hmm."

He tucked a strand of her hair behind her ear. "What?"

She rubbed her nose against his. "You said it first."

"Do I get points for that?"

"You do. Lots of points."

He stroked his hands down her back to hold her bottom and rocked his hips, enjoying the way he slid easily inside her.

"Stop it, you're making squelchy noises," she complained.

He nibbled down her neck. "Squelchy noises are sexy."

"They're really not. You're disgusting."

"Yes I am, and I'm afraid that's something you'll have to get used to if we're going to make a go of this."

She lifted off him, grabbed a tissue from the box on the bedside table to dispose of the evidence, then lay on her side facing him and propped her head on a hand.

He did the same, mirroring her pose, and they studied each other quietly for a moment. The evening breeze ruffled the thin curtains at the windows and brought goose bumps rising on his skin. He'd have to close the windows soon, but the bar where they were obviously having a Christmas party was playing Mariah Carey's *All I Want for Christmas is You*, and it gave him such a happy feeling that he decided to wait until they were ready for sleep.

Erin was sucking her bottom lip, and his heart rate picked up a little. After what he'd declared, a conversation about their future was inevitable. He welcomed it, though, wanting to clarify their feelings for each other. Did she want a relationship with him?

Chapter Twenty-Four

Brock's expression held a glint of amusement, and Erin had the feeling he was waiting to see if she'd cave and break the silence first. She'd wondered whether he'd be worried that he'd told her he loved her, when she hadn't said it back. He didn't look worried though. If anything, he looked a little smug, obviously pleased he'd said it first.

She held out for as long as she could, then sighed and gave in. "You really want to make a go of it?"

He smiled. "Yes." He lifted a finger and traced along her shoulder. "I know it's not cool to be too intense, and I don't want to frighten you off, so I'll try not to go overboard. But I will say I'm crazy about you. And before you say it's too soon to say I love you, we've been talking for over a year now. I know it's not the same as being together, but it's not as if we met yesterday. When Matt told me the other day that Ryan was sick, I knew instantly that I had to see you, and make certain for myself that he was receiving the best care."

"It was lovely of you to visit." She leaned her cheek into his palm as he cupped it. "I really appreciated that gesture."

"Well I hope I brightened his day—he certainly brightened mine."

She nibbled her bottom lip. There was no point in holding back now. This was the moment where they set the wheels of their future in motion, so she might as well be honest. "Is looking after another man's child something you really want to do? You're a decent guy, so I know you'll probably say yes because it sounds like the right thing to say, but I want to know what you really think. Ryan and I are a package deal, and I've never had a relationship while he's been around. I don't know how to balance things—he has to come first, and I'd hate for that to come between us."

He lifted two fingers and pressed them against her lips. "Sweetheart, of course your son comes first. I wouldn't expect anything less. And of course I get that the two of you are a package. He's a great kid, and I'd love to be a part of his life. I wouldn't expect him to call me Dad, but if he did, I wouldn't hate it."

Erin swallowed hard as a lump formed in her throat. His smile broadened as he obviously saw her emotion. "I'm not fibbing," he said. "I mean it."

"I know." She looked at where her hand lay on the duvet, and picked at the embroidery.

He slid a finger under her chin and lifted it. "What is it?"

She didn't want to voice her biggest concern, and she looked away, out to the view. The sun had set now, and the fairy lights were tiny stars against the darkening sea and sky.

"Is this about money?"

She turned back to look at him, surprised. "What makes you say that?"

"The things you've said before. Tell me why it bothers you."

"I don't want to have an argument."

"Neither do I. So how about we don't?" He smiled again.

She rubbed her nose. "So if I say something you disagree with, you're not going to try to change my mind?"

He frowned. "That's a discussion, Erin, not an argument. I won't try to browbeat you, if that's what you mean. You're entitled to your opinion. That doesn't mean your opinion is right." A glint appeared in his eye.

She reminded herself that he hadn't gotten where he was by being weak and wussy. But they had to have this conversation, because she couldn't get past the issue, and if she couldn't get past it, their relationship wouldn't work.

She blew out a breath. "It's something my mum said."

"What did she say?" His voice carried a hint of steel.

"Well, two things really. That it's not possible for a man to be truly unselfish. And that you won't be able to ignore a niggling doubt that I'm after your money, and it will come between us."

A long silence followed.

Brock's face remained carefully blank. "I see," he said eventually.

Tears pricked Erin's eyelids. "I'm not saying I agree," she whispered, hoping he wasn't going to yell at her.

"With which bit?"

"Sorry?"

"Which bit don't you agree with?"

She sighed. "Before I elaborate, I think I should make you aware of my track record with men. It's not good, which is the main reason

THE PERFECT GIFT

my mother is protective of me, because she's had to pick up the pieces on more than one occasion. My first boyfriend cheated on me with my then best friend. All my other relationships have ended disastrously. And of course there's Jack." Against her will, her bottom lip trembled.

Brock ran a hand through his hair. "Wait here a minute." He got up, pulled on his briefs, and walked out of the room.

A tear trickled down her cheek, which she brushed away hastily. She needed to try to keep emotion out of this. Of course that was impossible, but if she broke down in tears she'd be unable to keep a clear head, and this was a very important moment—if not one of the most important of her life.

Where had he gone? She sat up, her arms around her knees, hoping he hadn't rung for a taxi to take her to the airport or something. Was he angry? Did he want her to go?

She was considering getting up to find him when he reappeared. He had a wine glass in each hand, and a pretty green bag dangled from his fingers. After pausing to close the windows, he climbed back onto the bed.

"Mint chocolates," he explained, holding out the bag and one wine glass to her. "I figured we were going to be here a while, and that we might need sustenance."

Erin pressed her hand to her lips. He sipped his wine and then tipped his head at her. "What?"

"I thought you might be calling a taxi."

That earned her an exasperated look. "You really think I'm so easily scared?" He plumped up the pillows, leaned back against the headboard, and crossed his legs. "Sweetheart, I'm telling you now, you're stuck with me. I'm not going anywhere. I'm aware we have a few things to talk through, and I'm going to sit here until you've told me everything. I promise I'll listen while you tell me what a terrible mother and partner you've been, and then I'll spend as long as it takes convincing you otherwise." He took another mouthful of wine and swallowed.

She bit her lip, fighting against a smile. He raised an eyebrow and helped himself to a mint chocolate. "Go on then. Off you go."

"I don't know what to say now."

"Tell me about Jack."

153

She drew up her knees and rested her chin on them, swirling the wine in the glass. "For most of my life, I haven't been the type of girl to draw a man's gaze." She ignored his snort of disdain. "I was always too tall, too gawky… All the good-looking men went for the sporty girls, the confident ones. Yeah I had a few boyfriends, but they were average guys, nice enough, but not the sort girls ogled in the street. Then I met Jack. He was like a movie star. Tall, dark, handsome, played rugby, slightly arrogant but in a confident, sexy way."

She stopped as Brock raised an eyebrow. "I'd like it if you could get to the part where he's an ass," he said.

"It's coming soon, believe me. I couldn't believe it when he asked me out. I had stars in my eyes—I'm embarrassed to admit it, but it's true. I felt such an idiot when he refused to acknowledge Ryan. It was the lowest point of my life. I considered everything—abortion, suicide. I just wanted the hurt to stop."

Brock reached out and took one of her hands in his. "But you didn't do either of those things. That says something for the strength of your character."

"I suppose. Oddly, in spite of everything that's happened to me, deep down I do believe a man can be altruistic. I know you didn't expect me to sleep with you at Paua Cliffs. Hoping and expecting are two different things."

His lips twisted. "I'm glad you realize that."

"I do," she said earnestly. "But the point is, I know I've had bad judgement in men, and that I trust too easily. I wear my heart on my sleeve and I don't think it's a good thing—I'm too sensitive, too vulnerable. I know I should question more and trust less. I should hold back rather than throw myself into everything blindly. That's what I'm trying to do here. To take a step back and think with my head and not my heart."

Brock lifted her fingers to his lips and kissed them. "I understand. I think there are two issues going on here. You've been badly hurt, and naturally that's made you wary of trusting anyone. The only thing I would say is that questioning your natural instincts and ignoring them are two different things."

"Maybe," she conceded. She waited for him to say the second issue was money.

"The other issue has been created by the first, and that's your low self-esteem."

She blinked. "Sorry?"

"You don't believe a man in my position, who—so you believe—could have any woman he wants, would choose you."

She opened and closed her mouth several times, then finally closed it as he raised an eyebrow. "Yeah," she said. "You may be right."

"I know I'm right. And I'll add that you're wrong on several accounts."

"I'm sure you'll enlarge upon them for me," she said wryly.

"I will." He motioned for her to drink her wine. "Firstly, you are making the assumption that money can buy everything. I acknowledge there are women out there who will date a guy for his money. Of course there are. But equally there are a good proportion of decent, honorable women who would be offended by that."

Erin picked at the embroidery on the duvet.

"Secondly," he continued, "if I could pick any woman in the world, why wouldn't I choose you? What don't you possess that other women have?"

A tear rolled down her cheek. Brock caught it on a finger and sighed. "The money is irrelevant. It's just something that allows me to live comfortably and help other people out. It's mine and I've earned it—most of it—and I don't see what's wrong with me spending it on whatever I like."

"There's nothing wrong with that," she said with a sniff.

"Thank you. So therefore you won't mind if I spend it on you and Ryan." He smiled.

She took another mouthful of wine and set the glass aside, wrapping her arms around her knees again. "The thing is, Mum asked me whether I could be certain that I'm not interested in you because being with you would make our lives easier, and… I feel awful because I can't deny that. I'm scared that one day, maybe after we have an argument or something, it will be something that comes between us."

"I would think it's perfectly natural for someone who's existed on a pittance to be attracted by the idea of having money. I'd be surprised if you *weren't* comforted by the notion of being able to provide better for Ryan—not that I think you've done a bad job so far. That's okay, Erin. I don't have my head up my arse enough to think money isn't a factor at all. But I would never blame you for it. I would never use that against you. Because I know you would never be with me just for my money. You do wear your heart on your sleeve, and I don't believe you'd be able to hide your true feelings for me."

He held out his hand, and this time she laid hers in it. "We have something special," he stated, "and have had from the first moment we talked online, all those months ago. And I'm not going to let your fears, or your mother, or anything else in fact, come between us."

"Doesn't it worry you that people you know will say I'm after your money?"

"The people I like wouldn't think that and certainly wouldn't say it. And I don't care what the people I don't like are thinking."

"Okay," she said softly.

"Do you believe me?"

"I believe you."

"Good." He pulled the hand he was holding so she fell against him. "Now come here and kiss me."

She snuggled up to him, drawing the duvet with her, and they kissed lazily for a while, his lips moving across hers with a tenderness that brought more tears to her eyes.

He lifted his head and kissed her nose. "There's no hurry, and I'm willing to wait as long as it takes, but you should know that I'd like you to consider moving in with me."

"Here? In Auckland?"

"We'll talk about it, but that's one option. Either here, or maybe it would be nicer to get a house with a garden for Ryan. I know you're close to your parents and that you'd miss them if you moved here, but I'd be happy to fly them down regularly, or even help move them here if they'd like that. It's up to you. If you'd rather us just meet up at weekends for now, that's fine too."

Her mind spun. "I'll have to think about it."

"Of course. One more thing—I might have a job for you too."

"Goodness."

He laughed. "The hospital has a radio station—the biggest in the country. It's mainly run by volunteers, but we do have a paid position for the person overseeing the program. Ophelia, the woman who currently runs it, is leaving. You'd have to interview for it, of course, but I think you'd be perfect for the job. You have such a lovely voice and, with your background in publishing, I think you'd bring a lot to the role."

She couldn't take it all in. "What about Ryan?"

"There's a daycare facility just down from the hospital."

"It… it sounds perfect."

He smiled. "I'm glad."

"I'd like to think about it though, if that's okay."

"Of course. I don't expect you to make a decision now. In the meantime, though, I'm having a party on Christmas Eve, and I'd love it if you could come."

"A dinner party?"

"No, more relaxed than that. My parents and brothers will be there, and a few friends from work. Your parents are welcome to come too. I've cut myself off from life over the past two years, and I want to reconnect. It seems like a good time to start."

"Okay. I'll come. Can I let you know my decision about Auckland then?"

"There's no time limit, sweetheart. I'll be here when you feel ready."

He pushed her shoulder to turn her onto her side away from him. She rolled over, and he pulled her back into his arms. "Sleep tight, honey."

In spite of everything he'd told her, her eyelids were already drooping. "You too."

Her mind continued to whirl, but Brock's slow, regular breathing comforted her, and eventually she let sleep take her away.

*

When the sun came up the next morning, she opened sleepy eyes and a smile spread across her face.

Ryan had come into the room looking for her after rousing at three o'clock. She'd taken him to the bathroom, poured him a glass of water, and tried to settle him again, but he'd been unnerved by the strange surroundings and had clung to her, sucking on Dixon's paw.

Brock had come in to find them, and told her to bring him into their bed. She'd hesitated, not wanting to set a precedent, but his smile had been warm and genuine, and in the end she'd carried the boy in and settled him between them, and all three of them had dozed off again in minutes.

Now, Ryan lay on his side facing away from Brock, but he was snuggled up against the man's chest. Brock's arm rested across the boy, his hand holding Dixon tightly to Ryan's tummy. The two of them looked contented and cozy, so much so it brought a pain to her chest.

Was it possible she had at last found herself a decent guy? Someone who'd care for her and her son, who'd treat the boy as his own, and who'd make sure she never wanted for anything again?

Had she really been given the perfect gift for Christmas?

Chapter Twenty-Five

The festive season had always been a busy time at the hospital in the past, and this year proved to be no exception.

As usual, Brock spent the few days leading up to Christmas diagnosing and caring for sick kids and reassuring their parents, but he had to admit that lately he felt more than his standard sympathy for the worried mums and dads and the ill children. Now, he saw Ryan in every coughing boy and Erin in the concerned face of every parent. For the first time, when Erin rang him two days later to say she'd caught Ryan's second asthma attack of the year just in time, he really understood what those parents had been going through.

He asked her to fly down to Auckland immediately, but she reassured him they were fine, and she'd be there on Christmas Eve for the party in a few days. He didn't argue with her, knowing he had to let her come to a decision about their relationship in her own time.

He wasn't used to waiting, though, and he didn't like it one bit. He wanted Erin by his side so he could comfort and reassure her, and he wanted Ryan there so he could keep an eye on him. He told Erin as much, flatly and without mincing his words, not ashamed to tell her how he felt. She thanked him and said she was touched by his concern, but ended the call soon after that, leaving him wondering if he'd somehow upset her.

Two days passed, during which they had trouble connecting, one of them always in the middle of something each time the other rang. Brock was either in clinic or seeing to patients and had to ignore the buzz of a call from the phone in his pocket, and each time he called her back, she was in the middle of the supermarket or bathing Ryan or had her mother there and couldn't talk.

Their conversations weren't exactly stilted, but they didn't hold the warm affection he'd grown to love. He missed her, but he was beginning to worry she'd decided she didn't want to make the move to Auckland.

"You did say you'd move to the Bay if she wanted?" It was Matt who asked the question on Skype, the night before Christmas Eve, when the three of them had their usual weekly catchup.

"I forgot," Brock said. "I thought she'd get swept away with the notion of being by my side permanently. I didn't consider she might not see it as an attractive proposition."

"I'm sure she does," Charlie said, for once not picking up on Brock's attempt to make light of the situation. "It was easy to see the connection between the two of you online, and it sounds as if you got on well in the flesh."

"Yeah," Brock said, the word 'flesh' conjuring up visions of Erin's pale silky thighs and bare breasts.

"Earth to Brock?" Charlie said.

"What?"

"Your eyes have glazed over. Stop thinking about her naked. We're talking about serious relationship stuff here."

"I know. That's sort of the problem. I said the three little words and I'm not sure I should have."

"Did she say them back?" Matt asked.

"Nope."

The three of them fell quiet for a moment. Brock looked at his brothers' faces—Charlie's concerned eyes behind his dark-rimmed glasses, Matt's frown beneath his spiky fringe. They were worried about him, and that wasn't fair, not on the eve of Christmas.

"What is this," he joked, "are we all turning into girls? Want to paint each other's toenails and braid our hair?"

"Yeah," Matt said sarcastically. "Let's get out the beer and fart to the National Anthem."

Charlie rolled his eyes. "Stop avoiding the issue. What are you going to do about Erin?"

Brock shrugged. "Not much I can do. She's coming down tomorrow, and I have a feeling she'll have an answer for me then. I can only wait."

"That sucks."

"Yeah."

"We three Kings don't do waiting."

Brock gave a short laugh. "Not normally, no. In this case, though, there isn't an option. Anyway, are you guys still coming to the party?"

They both nodded.

"Bringing a plus one?"

"Might be," they both said at the same time, and laughed.

Brock grinned. "Might be or will be?"

"Depends," Matt said.

"On what?"

"If she's still talking to me."

"Like that is it?"

Matt shrugged. "What about you?" he said to Charlie. "How are things going there?"

Charlie pulled a face. "Touch and go."

"Jeez." Brock sighed. "We're not doing great, are we?"

"We rely on you to set an example," Matt pointed out.

"Fair enough. But you never know, maybe tomorrow night we'll all get our heart's desire."

Charlie and Matt both looked doubtful.

"Yeah," Brock said. "It's a long shot. Still, it is Christmas."

*

The day of the party dawned bright and sunny. Brock left the arrangements in the care of the event planning company he'd hired and spent the morning and early afternoon at the hospital. The last couple of years he'd offered to work over Christmas so the consultants with families could have a few days off, but this year he finished up around three p.m. and headed home. Erin was arriving at the airport at five with Ryan and her parents, and Brock had arranged for Lee to pick them up, so they'd be at the apartment by five thirty. Everyone else was arriving around six.

That gave him a couple of hours to make sure everything was ready. As soon as he walked into the apartment, though, he saw that there wasn't going to be a lot for him to do. The party organizers had strung fairy lights throughout the rooms and placed elegant center pieces made from fresh flowers and Christmas decorations on all the tables. Trays of wine glasses stood ready on the kitchen counter, while staff were heaping platters with cold nibbles and preparing hot ones ready for the oven. They'd filled the fridge with various white wines and the liquor cabinet held all manner of spirits and other drinks for those who preferred something different. It promised to be a great party—but deep inside, Brock knew he would judge the success of the evening by what Erin had to say.

He hoped that if she intended to either break it off or say she wanted to slow things down that she would have told him over the phone—hopefully the fact she was still coming, and bringing her parents, meant she still wanted to see him, and maybe even discuss moving things forward, but he couldn't be sure.

After chatting to the head of the event planning company to make sure she didn't need anything, he went into his bedroom and shut the door.

For a moment, he just stood there, looking at the bed and remembering the previous weekend, where he'd made love to Erin in that beautiful silky nightie, when she'd promised she'd let him do whatever he wanted to her. When he thought about it, they'd only slept together a few times. Was he crazy to be pressing her into a serious relationship when they hadn't known each other for very long?

Even as he formed the question, he rolled his eyes and discarded it. He had no doubts whatsoever that he wanted to spend the rest of his life with her. All that remained was to wait and see if she felt the same.

He opened the windows to let the afternoon breeze in, then lay on the bed and picked up his phone. Erin would be getting ready to go to the airport, if she wasn't there already.

He dialed her number and got her answerphone.

Sighing, he typed a text. *Are you at the airport yet? Miss you! B xx* and sent it. Then he lay back and picked up his iPad to flick through some notes from work he'd promised himself he'd finish before the party.

He couldn't concentrate, though, and eventually he put the iPad down and stared up at the ceiling.

For the first time in a few days, he thought of his sister. If Pippa hadn't died, she would have been twenty-five, and no doubt she would have come to his party and loved every minute of it. Then again, maybe he wouldn't have had a party if she hadn't died. If she hadn't had a fatal asthma attack, he and his brothers wouldn't have felt the need to work so hard developing their medical equipment, and although they hadn't exactly been poor to start with, they probably wouldn't be as rich as they were now.

Or would they? All three of them were ambitious and hardworking. Maybe they would just have funneled that energy in another direction. He couldn't imagine any world where Charlie didn't have his head buried in test tubes and equipment, or where Matt wasn't sketching and painting. Matt would have just ended up doing another series of children's books, and Charlie would have invented some other amazing thing that nobody had thought of before.

And what about himself? Brock sighed. Even if Pippa had survived, Fleur would still have died. He'd still be alone.

Would he have been a doctor? There was no doubt that Pippa's passing had driven him into medicine, but he couldn't imagine doing anything else now. He loved his job, loved helping people, so in that sense he had to be grateful that at least something positive had come out of her death.

Closing his eyes, he imagined what life would have been like if both Pippa and Fleur had survived. He would have had his sister and wife. But he'd never have met Erin.

A year ago, he would have given his whole fortune and everything he owned to have Fleur back. But now, the thought of being without Erin made his throat tighten.

He lifted his hands and sank them into his hair. *You don't have to choose*, he told himself, swallowing hard to try to get his throat to relax. When Fleur had died, he'd gotten off one train and crossed the station to get on another. The first train had gone no further, whereas the second train had set off on another set of tracks. There had been no choice to make. He'd had to keep going, and he was extremely lucky in that he'd found another woman as beautiful in both body and spirit as his first wife.

He pictured Pippa in his mind. *Please make her come to the party*, he begged. *I love her so much. Please make her come.*

On the bed beside him, his phone pinged, announcing the arrival of a text. Opening his eyes, he picked the phone up and swiped the screen. It was from Erin.

I'm on the plane. See you soon! E xxxx

A smile spread across his face, the wave of emotion so strong it made tears prick his eyes. He sniffed, hit reply, and sent a message back. *Have a safe journey. How are your parents?*

They're fine, thanks, she replied. *Looking forward to the party.*

And how's the boy doing? Excited?

Super-excited. Did I mention I'm on the plane? I'm supposed to turn my phone off.

He grinned. *One more minute. I miss you, sweetheart. Can't wait to see you again.*

Me too. Now Pat's glaring at me. Stop texting me!

I'm lying on the bed and thinking about Saturday night.

OMG! Stop it! I'm turning my phone off now. xxxxxx

He laughed and put the phone down. Half of him wanted to run yelling through the apartment. The other half wanted to bawl like a toddler.

Deciding neither was the best bet, he blew out a long breath and sat up. *Thanks*, he said silently to Pippa.

Erin was on her way, and now it was time to get ready for the party. Whistling *Jingle Bells*, he walked over to his wardrobe and opened the door.

He stopped whistling when he saw the gift sitting on the shelf to the side. A tiny box with a red bow on top.

For a long moment, he perused it, then he turned his gaze away. He took out a pair of black jeans and pulled them on, and chose the new light gray dress shirt with the fine black velvet swirls on it he'd bought for the party.

His gaze returned to the box while he buttoned up his shirt. When he'd done, he pursed his lips and huffed a sigh, his hands on his hips.

Go on, Pippa said in his head.

Lips curving up, he took the box, slid it into the pocket of his jeans, and headed out of the room.

Chapter Twenty-Six

Ryan pressed his nose against the wall of the elevator and breathed out, misting up the mirror.

"Don't make a mess," Karen Bloom said nervously, pulling him away and scrubbing at the steamy patch with her bag.

Erin smiled, knowing Brock wouldn't give a damn about misted-up mirrors or sticky fingerprints. The thought gave her a little glow inside.

It was strange to see her mother on edge and nervous, for once. Usually Erin was the one who Karen had to comfort and reassure. Erin decided she rather liked it being this way around.

She hadn't felt this confident all week. When she'd gone back to Kerikeri, she'd been full of conflicting emotions, from excitement that he'd asked her to move in with him, to sheer panic at the thought of what her mother and everyone else would say.

She'd kept the news to herself for a few days, hugging it to her like a cushion, knowing that all the while she didn't tell anyone, she could pretend everything was going to be all right and it would all work out fabulously. Deep down, though, her mother's words about Brock eventually accusing her of being after his money had continued to eat away at her, even though he'd promised he'd never say anything like that.

And then Ryan had suffered from his second asthma attack in as many weeks. Luckily she knew what to look for now, and they'd been at home so she'd been able to keep him relaxed enough to use his inhaler and spacer without panicking. By the time the ambulance arrived it was all under control, and they'd praised her on her level-headedness and ability to remain calm.

When they'd gone, though, and Ryan had finally fallen into an exhausted sleep, she'd allowed herself a few tears of relief, and it was then that Brock had rung her. She'd done her best to hide the fact that she was crying, but his words had grown clipped and curt as he'd demanded to know what had happened. For a moment, she'd thought he was angry with her for not going to the hospital, and she'd been prepared to announce hotly that she didn't want him telling her what to do.

Then he'd said, "I don't like that we're two hundred miles away. I want you here, with me. I want to check Ryan and see for my own eyes that he's okay. I can't hold you and comfort you from down here." His anger had come from the frustration of not being able to help, and from his love for her, and at that point it was all she could do to say goodbye and get him off the phone before she burst into great, gulping sobs.

He loved her, and he wanted her to move in with him. He was the nicest man she'd ever met, strong, capable, gorgeous, caring, and she was absolutely crazy about him. And at that moment, she knew she didn't care what anyone else said—not her mother, her father, or any of her friends—about her being after his money, because it simply wasn't true. She'd have loved him if he was penniless and lived in a hovel. It made no difference where they lived or what he spent on her or Ryan. She loved him, and that was all that mattered.

The elevator pinged, and the doors slid open. Before she could stop him, Ryan went running down the corridor—straight into the arms of the guy waiting at the end.

"Hey!" Brock swung the boy up into the air. "It's my favorite dude!"

"Bwock!" Ryan flung his arms around the man's neck and squeezed him tight enough to cut off his circulation. "I've come to your party."

"Thank God you've arrived. It wouldn't have been a party at all without you."

Smiling, Erin beckoned to her parents to follow her and walked along the corridor to them. "Hey, you," she said, lifting her face to Brock when she reached him.

"Hello gorgeous." He dipped his head and touched his lips to hers for a long kiss. They were interrupted by Ryan, who pressed his face in between theirs to join in with the kiss.

Laughing, they broke apart. Erin turned and held her hand out to her parents. "Brock, you remember my mum, Karen."

"Of course I do. I'm so glad you came." He held out the hand not supporting Ryan to her, and she clasped it with a smile.

"Hello, Brock. Thank you so much for inviting us."

"You're very welcome."

"This is an amazing apartment."

"I'll show you around in a moment." Brock held out a hand to the man waiting beside her. "You must be Erin's father. Nice to meet you."

"It's Pete, and likewise." The two men shook hands. "Thanks for the trip in the jet," Pete added. "I never want to fly with people again!"

Brock laughed and headed into the living room. "I know what you mean—once you fly private, the idea of standing in a queue and then sitting in a cabin with thirty others isn't very appealing."

Erin watched her mother's eyes widen as they entered the living room. It looked beautiful with all the tasteful decorations and lights, and the magnificent view beyond.

"Oh my God." Karen pressed a hand to her heart. "Erin, it's even better than you described."

"Come on," Brock said, lowering Ryan to the ground. "I'll show you around."

Erin followed behind, listening to Brock as he talked to her parents while they walked slowly through the apartment. He'd told her that he had a firm organizing the party, and she nodded as they passed the staff who were preparing trays of food, trying to look as if she went to a catered party every day.

Inside, though, in spite of a flutter of nerves, her heart was swelling. Seeing Brock banished any last dregs of doubt, and all she could think was how wonderful it was to see him, and how she didn't want to leave him ever again. Ryan stuck like Velcro to his side, but Brock didn't look annoyed, just delighted to see the boy, and whenever they stopped walking and Ryan put his arms around him, Brock ruffled his hair or patted his back, and once bent to kiss the top of his head.

By the time they'd finished looking around and had returned to the living room, Erin knew it wouldn't be long before the rest of the guests started arriving.

"Mum," she said, "would you mind looking after Ryan? I want to talk to Brock for a moment."

Karen met her eyes and smiled. Erin had finally plucked up the courage to tell her what she'd decided, and to her pleasure Karen hadn't queried her decision, but had just nodded and said she'd known that was coming, because she'd not seen Erin as happy as this for many years.

"Come on Ryan, Brock's left you some coloring pencils on the coffee table," Karen told him, and she and Pete led the boy to the table by the Christmas tree, where Brock had thoughtfully placed several Ward Seven coloring books next to some tiny crust-free sandwiches and crisps for the boy.

Erin watched them go, then turned to find Brock where he was in a discussion with the party planner. For a moment, Erin just looked at him, enjoying the view. His black jeans were tight on his bum and emphasized his long legs, while the dress shirt looked smart and summery at the same time. He'd rolled up his shirt sleeves a little, and in true Kiwi style he had bare feet, which made her smile.

At that moment he turned, catching her smile, and his lips curved in response. After finishing off his conversation, he walked across to her. "What are you smiling at?"

"You." She held out a hand and, when he grasped it, led him out through the open sliding doors onto the deck. It was a gorgeous, warm evening, the beautiful red of the sky caused by the sinking sun a Christmas decoration all of its own.

"How are you doing?" he asked, turning her to face him and sliding his arms around her.

"I'm good." She placed her hands on his chest, enjoying the feel of firm muscles beneath her fingertips.

"And how's Ryan?"

"Better, thanks."

"I'm glad. I've worried myself sick all week."

She kissed his cheek. "You're so sweet."

"And you're so sexy." He nuzzled her ear. "You look gorgeous tonight."

"Thank you." Her cheeks glowed with the compliment. Karen had given her some money for Christmas and told her to go out and buy herself something. Caitlin had accompanied her, and helped her to choose a flowing light blue skirt that reached to just above her knees, with a pretty blue-and-pink vest to wear with it. "It's pretty, isn't it?"

"It shows off your breasts nicely," he agreed.

She laughed. "Thank you for noticing."

"Oh, I can safely say I can always be relied upon to notice what your breasts look like."

Smiling, she kissed him briefly, then moved back and lifted a hand to cup his cheek. "I have something to say to you."

He took a deep breath in and then let it out slowly, as if he was preparing himself for bad news. "Okay."

She looked into his lovely brown eyes. "I love you."

His eyes widened. "Oh."

"I should have said it last weekend, Brock, and I'm so sorry I didn't. I've been scared and worried and concerned about everything except what really matters—that you love me, and I love you. I've missed you all week, and what you said on the phone, about wanting to be near me so you could look after me—"

"I thought I'd overdone it," he said hoarsely. "I didn't mean to sound overbearing and controlling."

"It's okay." She stroked his cheek. "I love that you care, and that you want to look after us. And I'm not going to feel bad because that makes me feel good, you know? I'm not going to feel guilty for looking at the bigger picture, and for feeling grateful that I've found a guy who's not only gorgeous and sexy and great in bed, but who wants to care for me. I can look after myself, I've proved that, but I love the idea of being able to share everything with someone for a change."

His eyes glistened. "Me too."

"I've told my parents. And if the offer's still there, I'd love to move in with you."

"Of course the offer's still there," he said softly, tightening his arms around her.

"I love the sound of the job too, and I'd like to interview for it."

"Do you want to live here, in this apartment?"

"I don't care, Brock. I really don't. I just want to be with you, and so does Ryan. All he's done is talk about you. He's almost as crazy about you as I am."

He chuckled and wrapped his arms around her, and she pressed her nose into his shirt, inhaling the scent of spicy body wash and warm male. "You've made me the happiest man alive, do you know that?"

"I'm so glad." She couldn't explain how safe she felt in his arms, and how much she wished she could stay there all night. "I love you."

"I love you too," he said, holding her so tightly she felt quite breathless.

She wriggled, feeling something pressed against her hip. "Have you got something in your pocket, or are you just pleased to see me?"

"Oh. I... ah..." He moved back and looked down at her, but at that moment the sound of a bell announced the arrival of someone in the elevator. "Damn it. It'll have to wait."

"What will?"

"Nothing. I expect it's Charlie. He's always first and has no idea about being fashionably late. Or fashionably anything, in fact."

She laughed. "I'll get Ryan." Glowing inside, she crossed the room to retrieve her son.

*

Brock watched her go, pausing on the edge of the room and sliding his hands into the pockets of his jeans. His fingers closed around the little velvet box, and he squeezed it tight.

There was no rush. He'd welcome his guests and wait until the party was in full swing. Then he'd take her somewhere quiet, pop the question, and hope Christmas had a little magic left for him.

Smiling, he held out his hand as she rejoined him with Ryan, and they walked across the room to welcome their guests.

*

Continue the story of the Three Wise Men in Charlie and Ophelia's story, *An Ideal Present (Three Wise Men Book 2)*

Sneak Peek at Chapter One of An Ideal Present

"I feel as if I've stepped into *Invasion of the Body Snatchers*," Ophelia said with a smile.

The doctor in the white coat paused in the process of paying for his muffin and looked over the top of his dark-framed glasses at her. His frown suggested confusion rather than amused interest, as she'd hoped.

In the background, someone was playing Eartha Kitt's *Santa Baby* in their office. She fought the urge to sing it to him, not sure it would help her situation, and tapped the paper bag in his hand. "Since when have you ever bought a savory muffin? You always pick sweet. Blueberry or chocolate usually. Clearly, you're a duplicate from an alien seed pod."

Okay, so maybe it wasn't the funniest joke in the world, but she'd expected a polite smile if nothing else. The frown remained in place, however. Either he thought her sense of humor severely lacking, or she'd weirded him out with her observation of his baked goods.

"Sorry," she mumbled, admitting defeat. Grimacing, she turned on her heel and walked back through the corridors to the wing of the hospital where she worked.

Once inside, she tossed her bagel onto her desk, flopped into her chair, and stared at the clock. Ten thirty. Far too early to admit the day was doomed and go home.

She blew out a long breath. Was she really surprised the cute doctor hadn't laughed at her joke? How long had they been meeting at the snack cart—nearly a year? And he'd barely said two words to her in all that time that didn't involve food or the weather. Clearly, he wasn't interested, and it was about time she took the hint.

She leaned forward and covered her face with her hands. It was irrelevant anyway. She was hardly in the right place to start seeing someone. She might have been separated from her husband since June, but it had proved surprisingly difficult to extricate herself from the emotional ties to her ex.

It didn't help that even though Dillon had moved out, he was always at the house. She felt as if she couldn't object—he was either seeing their daughter, which of course he had every right to do, or carrying out the occasional bit of building work to improve the house for when they put it up for sale. But she knew it was all a pretense, because he'd made it quite clear that although he was willing to let her have some time apart, he didn't want the marriage to end.

"You'll always be my girl," he'd said to her only a few weeks ago when he'd tried to persuade her to go out to dinner with him for his birthday. She'd declined, but she'd felt bad about it. When he'd moved out, she'd thought it would draw a line under their marriage, and her emotions might finally be able to level out after the rollercoaster ride she'd been on for well over a year. But six months later, she still felt torn in two every time she saw him. He represented comfort and security, which were not to be sniffed at. She knew every little thing about him and in many ways that was reassuring in a relationship. He was Summer's father, and of course Summer would prefer the two of them to stay together. And it wasn't as if he had some immense flaw that had forced them apart—he wasn't an alcoholic or a gambler, he was a good looking guy, and he was decent in bed.

And yet all the million-and-one tiny reasons that had driven her to tell him it was over were still there. The jealousy, the possessiveness, the superior way he had of talking to her occasionally as if she was stupid, the nasty, cruel side of him that only came through when they argued. She knew that if she asked him to move back home, the first time they had an argument and he twisted her words the way he always did, she would regret her decision, and it would be even harder to convince him to leave a second time.

Then she thought of Summer, who missed her daddy, and her throat tightened.

She swallowed hard. She'd made the right choice, and this was one of the very few cases where she felt she had to put herself first if she didn't want to spend another year feeling miserable and depressed. Being on her own was scary, but she shouldn't let that be the reason she stayed with Dillon. It would be worse for Summer if her parents remained together but argued all the time.

She'd known him since they were in high school, and he'd been her first real boyfriend. For seven years, she'd compromised and negotiated her way through their marriage until she'd forgotten who she was and what she wanted. She needed time alone, a fresh start, to rediscover the Ophelia that hopefully still existed beneath the mum and wife. The last thing she needed was to start dating again.

Sighing, she lowered her hands, ready to start work. Then she inhaled sharply at the sight of the cute doctor leaning against the doorjamb, watching her.

"Oh." She stared at him, stunned into silence. He'd never once come to this part of the hospital. And it didn't look as if he was here on business. He didn't march up to her desk and give her any paperwork. He didn't speak. He didn't even smile. He just stood there, leaning, watching her.

"I'm sorry about the alien joke," she said, wondering if he'd come to tell her off. "It sounded funnier in my head."

"It *was* funny," he said. His deep, gravelly voice sent a shiver down her spine. "I just thought you were comparing me to the duplicates in the story."

She blinked. As far as she remembered, the alien duplicates had been devoid of all human emotion. "What do you mean? Why would I compare you to them?"

"It wouldn't be the first time."

She wasn't sure what to make of that. "Well, I wasn't. It was purely a muffin-based gag."

He nodded, although he still didn't smile. Then he raised the hand not holding the paper bag with his muffin. He touched the top button of his coat. Slowly, he popped it through the buttonhole, then continued down until all the buttons were undone. Once the white coat hung open, he flicked back the side of it and slid his hand into the pocket of his well-worn jeans.

Aware that her jaw had dropped at his pseudo-striptease, Ophelia closed her mouth and took the opportunity to admire him. She estimated he was maybe six-three or four, but it was the geeky scientist look he sported that tended to draw her attention rather than his height, with his dark-rimmed rectangular glasses, longish, slightly scruffy hair, and vacant look, as if he was constantly trying to calculate the value of pi to a thousand decimal places in his head.

He looked like the kind of guy who might have worn a faded T-shirt under his coat with the logo of some nerdy computer game, but to her surprise he wore one of the performance-fit All Blacks rugby tops, and it clung to an impressively flat abdomen and a broad, muscular chest. She hadn't expected that, either. He didn't look the type who spent hours at the gym, but there were definitely muscles showing through the clingy fabric.

His jeans were tight, too, emphasizing muscular thighs that could squeeze a girl to death. Well-worn Converses finished the look, giving him an air of casual indifference. He didn't care what he wore, but it didn't stop him wearing it well.

She lifted her gaze back up to his face. Now he looked slightly nonplussed, as if the reason for her lazy perusal eluded him. He had no idea how sexy he looked.

"What can I do for you?" she asked softly.

He pushed himself off the doorjamb and walked toward her desk. "I hear you're leaving."

He knew she was leaving?

Wait, he knew who she was?

Act cool, Ophelia. She leaned forward, intending to rest her chin on her hand, but her elbow missed the table and she almost fell off her chair. He raised an eyebrow.

Face burning, she leaned back and cleared her throat. "Yes. Second week in January."

To her surprise, he pushed the contents of the corner of her desk into the middle and sat on the edge. "Why?"

Ophelia tried not to stare at the jumble of spilled pens and paper clips that rested very near his muscular thigh. "I have a new part-time job nearer to my daughter's school. She has—"

"Cystic Fibrosis, yeah I know," he said. "How is she?"

Her jaw dropped. Until now, she'd assumed he hadn't even known she existed. How was he aware of her daughter's condition? "Um, she's had a few chest infections this year, so her doctor recommended I start upping her physiotherapy sessions to three times a day. It's just too far to travel from here to see her at lunch time."

"Fair enough." He looked at the ground for a moment. Then, to her surprise, he slid his glasses off, folded them, and slipped them into his top pocket before looking at her.

She inhaled slowly, entranced by his beautiful deep brown eyes. Wow, the guy was gorgeous. Yes, there was something slightly geeky about him, but after being married to a rough-and-ready builder for seven years she found his gentle manner and intelligence incredibly attractive.

He studied her face for a long moment, and she realized that whereas a blank expression on Dillon's face tended to indicate an absence of thought, in this guy it meant he was contemplating what to say.

"What are you doing this evening?" he asked eventually.

It was such a clumsy question that it took a few seconds for her to understand what was going on.

Slowly, her lips curved up in a smile. "Um... I've nothing planned."

"Okay. I wondered if you and your daughter would like to come out for a drink. Well, obviously, your daughter wouldn't like an alcoholic drink, but maybe we could go to, I don't know, McDonald's or something, and she could have one of those Happy Meal things. You know, with a toy."

He looked alarmed at his inability to express himself, as if he couldn't stop his mouth from moving, and the words were just tumbling out.

"Are you asking me on a date?" she said, trying not to chuckle.

He scratched the back of his neck. "Apparently it's difficult to tell."

That made her laugh. He was so sweet. She felt as if they were fifteen and he was trying to ask her to the school ball.

Briefly, an image of Dillon flashed in her mind, and she felt a flicker of guilt at how hurt he'd be if she dated anyone else. And hadn't she just told herself she needed some time alone?

But the cute doctor's gaze rested on her, warm and interested, and her resolve melted. She and Dillon were separated and she'd made it quite clear she wanted their marriage to be over. It *was* over. Maybe going out with someone else would help her to move on.

"I didn't think you even knew who I was," she murmured.

He looked at the paper bag in his hand. "I don't like muffins."

"Sorry?"

"I don't eat them. Luckily my colleagues in research do."

He was telling her that he went to the snack cart so he could see her. Every day, for a year! Warmth spread through her as if she'd drunk a large glass of Scotch.

She smiled. "I'd love to go for a drink. I'm not sure I can get a babysitter at such short notice, though, so it might have to be McDonald's a little earlier, I'm afraid, if you want to make it today."

"That's great. I've always wanted to try a chicken nugget."

She raised her eyebrows. "You've never had chicken nuggets?"

"Nope. Never been to McDonald's. Or Burger King. Or Pizza Hut."

"Good Lord."

"I've been told I'm completely disconnected from modern civilization. I feel I should point this out now in case you'd rather back away while there's still time."

Was he being serious? *It wouldn't be the first time*, he'd said when referring to the alien duplicates, so clearly other people had struggled with his apparent lack of emotion. But his eyes were filled with warmth, and a gut feeling told her he just had an incredibly wry sense of humor that for whatever reason didn't reflect in his features. What a strange guy. And yet her life had been filled with worry and disappointment and sadness for so long that the thought of getting to know him better and injecting a little romance into her day brought a lightness to her heart.

"I'll risk it," she said.

Did she imagine it, or did his expression flicker briefly with relief? "Shall I pick you up from your house at, say, five? Or is that too late? I have no idea what time children go to bed."

"Five will be fine."

"Cool." He stood and attempted to help her rearrange the items he'd knocked over on her desk.

Their hands bumped, and her cheeks warmed. "It's okay, I'll do it," she said.

"Sure." He ran a hand through his hair and headed for the door.

"Hey," she called out, "I don't even know your name."

He stopped and turned around for a moment, shoving his hand back in his pocket. "Charlie," he said. "Charlie King. See you later." He walked away and disappeared around the corner.

Only then did she realize she hadn't told him where she lived. How would he know where to pick her up? It was really odd how he...

She blinked a few times. Wait a minute. Charlie King?

Her jaw dropped again. Brock, Charlie, and Matt King were three brothers who ran the company called Three Wise Men that designed medical equipment specifically for children.

Brock King was the consultant pediatrician specializing in respiratory diseases who'd first diagnosed her daughter with CF. Matt King had written a series of children's books called *The Toys from*

Ward Seven, and the new medical equipment was decorated with his characters, with the hoping of making it less scary for kids.

Charlie King was the brains behind the design. Ophelia knew that throughout the hospital he was famous for having an IQ that was one point off Einstein's. With Brock's help, it had been his invention of a revolutionary new asthma inhaler that had catapulted the company into success. All hospitals in New Zealand and a few in Australia now contained Three Wise Men equipment, and there was talk of expanding the business to Europe and maybe even America.

The fact that stunned her the most was connected to the charity called We Three Kings that the brothers ran. The charity funded research into respiratory diseases, and it paid for wishes to come true for terminally-ill children. It also had a website with chat rooms where parents of sick children could talk to each other, as well as ask advice of doctors out of hours. The site had grown from having a few hundred members to around fifty thousand, and many parents found it a comfort to keep in contact with others who were also struggling to cope with looking after sick kids.

The three brothers were known to go on there under pseudonyms, and Ophelia had spoken many times to Caspar—the name Charlie King used online. That's how he knew about her daughter. She hadn't mentioned leaving the hospital though, had she? So he must have asked around to discover that piece of information. He was quite flirty online—strange when he appeared to be so inept at it in real life!

She sat back in her chair, her mind whirling. A few months ago, the New Zealand Herald had published an article on the three King brothers, praising them for their ceaseless charity work, as the guys all visited hospitals dressed as Ward Seven characters to cheer up sick kids.

The article had also stated they were thought to be billionaires, and that all three of them were single. Since then, she was sure they'd been inundated with women hoping to snag a rich husband. They must get propositioned hundreds of times a day.

And yet Charlie had known who she was, and had come to ask her out.

Okay, McDonald's wasn't exactly the romantic destination she would have picked, but she was deeply touched that he hadn't assumed she'd just dump her daughter to go out with him. He'd included Summer in his plans, and that meant more to her than anything else he could have said or done.

Leaning on the table, she covered her mouth with her hands. She was going on a date with Charlie King, a gorgeous billionaire genius philanthropist who'd never eaten a chicken nugget in his life.

Oh my God. What was she going to wear?

Newsletter

If you'd like to be informed when my next book is available, you can sign up for my mailing list on my website, http://www.serenitywoodsromance.com

About the Author

Serenity Woods lives in the sub-tropical Northland of New Zealand with her wonderful husband and gorgeous teenage son. She writes hot and sultry contemporary romances and would much rather immerse herself in reading or writing romance than do the dusting and ironing, which is why it's not a great idea to pop round if you have any allergies.

Website: http://www.serenitywoodsromance.com
Facebook: http://www.facebook.com/serenitywoodsromance
Twitter: https://twitter.com/Serenity_Woods

Made in the USA
Monee, IL
26 October 2022

16586134R00103